Ghost

AT THE

Window

Ghost

AT THE

Window

Margaret McAllister

DUTTON CHILDREN'S BOOKS

New York

CENTRAL RESOURCE LIBRARY
LANCASTER COUNTY LIBRARY
LANCASTER, PA

This book is a work of fiction. Names, characters, places, and incidents are either the product of the author's imagination or are used fictitiously, and any resemblance to actual persons, living or dead, business establishments, events, or locales is entirely coincidental.

Copyright © 2002 by Margaret McAllister

All rights reserved. No part of this publication may be reproduced or transmitted in any form or by any means, electronic or mechanical, including photocopy, recording, or any information storage and retrieval system now known or to be invented, without permission in writing from the publisher, except by a reviewer who wishes to quote brief passages in connection with a review written for inclusion in a magazine, newspaper, or broadcast.

CIP Data is available.

Published in the United States by Dutton Children's Books,
a division of Penguin Putnam Books for Young Readers
345 Hudson Street, New York, New York 10014
www.penguinputnam.com

Designed by Richard Amari
Printed in USA
First Edition
ISBN 0-525-46852-8
1 3 5 7 9 10 8 6 4 2

CRL 15.99

For my sister Helen and for Tony and Helga,
all of whom have the gift of being there at the right time

Ghost

AT THE

Window

- 1 -

Ewan Dart was just leaving the post office when he overheard Mrs. Craigie talking to a customer.

"Ewan's not so bad himself, but his parents are an awful strange pair. I sometimes think it's the house that attracts them. Anyone who ever lived at Ninian House has been a wee bit odd, or fey, or just plain weird."

Ewan slipped out, feeling irritated and a bit pleased with himself at the same time. Irritated because Mrs. Craigie didn't know what she was talking about, and pleased because *he* did.

Ewan's parents *were* unusual and sometimes hard to live with, but they weren't weird—just artistic. It was the house itself—Ninian House—that was, as Mrs. Craigie had said, odd, or fey, or just plain weird.

The Scottish village of Loch Treen stood at one end of the long, narrow stretch of water it was named after. A single track road led between the rocky loch shore on one side and the low, rough hills. There were a few sparse, tough little trees, coarse heather and bracken, and, here and there, a cottage or a ruin. At the north end of the loch, rising on an outcrop of rock, stone-built and tall, stood Ewan's home, Ninian House. On a good day, with the sun glittering over the loch, it was the loveliest place to live. It could be the loneliest, too.

Long ago—more than a thousand years ago—a monk had lived there as a hermit. There had been a stone chapel, dedicated to St. Ninian, and a wooden hut. Later, a tower had been built on the site, and over the centuries the tower had become a small castle, and the castle had become a house.

At various times the house had been besieged or left to fall down, then rebuilt with any stone that could be found. Remains of farmhouses, leftovers from other crumbled towers, and stones from the Roman Wall and the ruins of Border abbeys were all in those walls. It had been attacked by armies and defended by warriors. Saints had prayed in it, fugitives had sheltered in it, lovers had escaped from it. Not surprisingly, the house sometimes forgot which century it was in. Ewan could be quietly doing his homework when suddenly everything around him would take a step back in time.

As he walked home along the loch side, Ewan kicked a pebble and wondered what his home would be doing when he got there. He might walk into a dim Victorian parlor, with ornaments everywhere and heavy, dark furniture draped in green bobbly cloths. Or he might find himself in a dark, poky shed with a haze of woodsmoke and a powerful smell of sheep. Or it could be a stone hall with gleaming swords and sturdy round shields piled up everywhere and big hairy warriors buckling on their war gear. Or it might only be his own home with his own parents in it—and that was strange enough.

Fortunately, when Ninian House slipped into another century, it never stayed there for long. He might walk into the wrong time, but the house seemed to find the right one in a matter of seconds, and the people he saw didn't notice him. They clearly couldn't see him, but he could see them, which made it a bit awkward if he wanted to invite anyone home.

This time, turning his key in the weighty old oak door and giving it a shove, he found a large, dark, drafty room. A woman by the hearth treadled steadily at a spinning wheel as it whirred, fleece twisting through her fingers. Then she vanished, and the hall was suddenly and brightly back to normal. Stacked-up paintings, multicolored throws, paint pots, and enormous colorful wall hangings surrounded him, and a twisted shopping cart stood lopsided in the middle of the floor.

His father ran down the stairs. His jeans, shirt, hands, and face were spattered with different shades of green and yellow paint. There were flecks of it in his hair, too, which was sticking up.

"Is it that time already?" he greeted Ewan. "You're home early. Watch out for the cart—I'm using it for a sculpture."

"I'm not early, Dad, I'm late," said Ewan. "I stopped at the post office to buy chocolate." He dumped his schoolbag on the floor, then thought better of it and picked it up again. Anything left lying around was likely to be painted and sent to a gallery. "I couldn't walk home with Mick today—his mum was taking him into town to buy shoes. I thought I'd cycle over there after dinner."

"We'll see what your mother thinks," said his father. Ewan's mother was anxious about him cycling long distances after dark.

"Where is she?" asked Ewan.

"She's doing some publicity photos somewhere. Somewhere near Ayr, I think. She'll be home—um—sometime or other." He looked at his hands as if he couldn't understand how the paint had gotten there, rubbed them on his shirt, then through his hair, and then went to wash up.

Ewan often wondered what it would be like to have ordinary parents. His father, Simon, was an artist and sculptor, and his mother was a photographer and style consultant who came home at any hour of the day or night, proclaiming, "Lilac and moss green will be absolutely *massive* this year!"

The house was a jumble of eras, colors, and accents. Simon was Welsh. Ewan's mother, Lizzie, came from Kent, in England, and Ewan had been born when they were living in the Scottish Borders. They had only lived in Ninian House for six months, ever since his father had gone to Loch Treen to paint and had seen it, empty and waiting to be bought. Ewan was never quite sure if he was English or Scots, so he had decided he was something in between—a Borderer.

He went up the wide stone stairs to his room. He always felt he should knock on his own bedroom door before opening it, in case somebody from the past was there. But today everything was as it should be, and he dumped his bag and changed out of his school sweater.

When he pulled the clean sweater over his head, he was definitely in his own bedroom. When he had wriggled it down over his ears, he wasn't.

There was a plain low bedstead covered in a patchwork quilt. A log fire was burning down to ashes in the grate, and there were no carpets, only a rag rug on the floor. Turning around, he saw a plain, heavy chest of drawers, a freestanding wardrobe—like his, only smaller—and a child's desk. The door of the closet in the wall, where he displayed his favorite football poster, was bare. A few old-fashioned toys lay on the chest—a pale-faced doll, a knitted rabbit, and a wooden spinning top. A hard-backed book lay open on the desk.

On the far side of the bed, something moved. Ewan, who had not noticed anyone there before, saw her now.

A girl stood beside the bed. She must have been eight or nine, perhaps—much younger than he. She was pale and red-haired and wore a long, plain, cream-colored shift that he supposed must be a nightgown. But what made her different from all the other strangers from the past—and made a shiver spread down his neck and all the way to his fingertips—was the way she was looking at him.

He told himself at first that she couldn't see him. None of them ever could. They just appeared, like people in a film. But with this one, there was no mistaking it. Her eyes were fixed on his face, and she looked so troubled, so sad and pleading, that her unhappiness made him hurt. She stretched out her hand toward him.

"Help me," she said. "Please, please. Help me."

- 2 -

What . . ." began Ewan, and stopped. It was too late.

He was in his own room again. The bed, with its multi-colored wildlife quilt, was his own. There was carpet under his feet, his own desk and chair were at one side of the window, his poster was on the closet door, and he was alone. He put both hands on the bed, to make sure that it felt right.

But she had been there. She had been real.

"Are you still there?" he said, and at once he felt silly, talking to empty space. He closed his eyes and opened them again, but it was still his own room. He tried going out, shutting the door, counting to five, and coming back in, but nothing changed, and he had the feeling—like ringing the doorbell of an empty house—that nothing would.

Outside, a car engine growled and stopped, and a door banged. Against the softness of browning heather and the silver-gray loch, his mother's sleek red car looked as if it, too, was in the wrong century. Ewan went to meet her, but as he closed the bedroom door behind him, he glanced back over his shoulder, just in case.

Dad, as usual when he was working, hadn't even thought about an evening meal, which meant that it would be something quick out of the freezer again. This time it was fish fingers and microwave French fries, and Mum parked a bit of parsley on the top because she said it made a bold and striking effect when combined with tomato sauce.

"Mum," said Ewan, "we don't know much about the people who lived here before, do we? I don't just mean the last people, I mean further back. We see them, but we don't know anything about them."

"I suppose you could find out," she said airily. She was concentrating on drawing Celtic knot patterns with her fork in a puddle of tomato sauce. "How far back do you mean?"

"I'm not sure. Not very long." He described to her the room he had seen, but he didn't tell her about the girl.

"From the bed, and the style of the coverlet," she said, "it could be sometime in the early twentieth century. Perhaps not all that early." She stopped drawing and gazed past him, and he could see she was trying to picture it with a professional eye. "Between the wars. I can't be sure without seeing it, but possibly nineteen twenties or thirties." She murmured something about art deco and went on, "I wish I'd seen that. I never get anything later than Victorian, with all those dramatic dark drapes and heavy prints. Although there was some truly stunning William Morris wallpaper in the sitting room—the colors just *sing* to you. Have you seen it?"

"Yes, Mum," said Ewan patiently, "but I want to know about the people, not the wallpaper. Can we find out who lived here?"

She shrugged. "Ask Mick's granny. She'll know if anyone does."

After the usual negotiations about what time to be home, and a reminder to "be sure to phone the minute you get there so I know you haven't fallen in the loch," Ewan cycled away along the loch-side path. It was a rough ride and a bumpy one, but he could make it in ten minutes. The lights of Mick's solid white cottage shone a welcome to him from far off, lights that appeared and disappeared as they were switched on and off with the continuous movement in Mick's house. That house was as welcoming as it looked, but it was a long way away. It might be the nearest house, but it wasn't in any sense "near" at all.

As Ewan wheeled his bike up the path and leaned it against the wall, he could already hear the rough, loud challenge of a barking dog. There was a cry of "Shut up, Bruce!" from one of Mick's sisters.

"Dogs and bairns, who'd have them!" exclaimed Mick's mum as she answered the door. She was round, kind, and sensible. "Come away in, Ewan." Mick's little sisters, Ruth and Sally, peeped around a door, giggled at him, and ran away, which was what they always did. Bruce was a

Labrador and a pretty good match for Mick. They were both dark and glossy-haired and made friends easily. Mick had a grin too big for his face, and Bruce had a bark too big for anyone. In Mick's room, Bruce sat and watched the remote-controlled car whiz past his nose as the two boys veered it around the floor.

"I saw this little kid in my bedroom today," said Ewan carelessly. "Except that she wasn't really there. You know what I mean."

Mick kept his eyes on the car as it careered up a ramp and stalled. "Your house is weird," he said. "It's very nice, but it's weird." He passed the controls to Ewan. "Your turn."

"I really like being at your house," said Ewan, and it wasn't just because of Mick and the remote-controlled car. He loved the ordinariness of Mick's home. Mick's dad worked at the council offices, and his mum looked after the family, the chickens, a few sheep, the holiday cottage next door, and her Granny Carmichael, who lived with them. For Loch Treen, that was normal.

"This little lass I was telling you about," Ewan said. "She talked to me."

"What did she say?"

"Not much, and then she vanished," replied Ewan, who was beginning to regret having mentioned her. In Mick's untidy room, with the big, silly dog watching the car like a spectator at a tennis match, it seemed impossible to believe that he had seen anyone in his room. If he had, there wasn't much to tell, but Mick was one of the few people he could talk to about the house.

That was something about Loch Treen. It had its own set of rules. People lived there because they wanted peace, mountains and water, and a quiet life. What they did not want was a lot of television crews and ghost-hunting nutcases traipsing about with cameras and crystals. Nobody minded what Ninian House did, as long as it did it quietly. Ewan suspected that local people who had been around for a long time—like Mick's mum and her family—had a pretty good idea of what Ninian House was really like, but they never mentioned it, and neither did he. It was as if the house occasionally made rude noises, but they all politely ignored them.

Perhaps, just for this evening, he should say no more about the strange child in his room. Looking out the window, he could see the lights were on in the smaller, whitewashed cottage behind Mick's house.

"Have you still got visitors in your holiday cottage?" he said.

"They're only there until the end of the week, and they're the last ones this year. Mum doesn't like it being empty all winter, but the holiday season's nearly over."

"That's a shame," said Ewan.

"No, it isn't. She says we can put up the snooker table in there and use it as a game room."

"Brilliant!" said Ewan as the car turned over on its roof. But it was growing dark and late, and soon it was time to leave Mick and Bruce, and their shabby, kindly home, and cycle back to Ninian House. His mother was hanging enormous bunches of creamy yellow dried flowers in the hall, and bits of twig had lodged themselves in her hair.

"I made these up for the Duchess of Etive," she said. "I had some left. Don't they look completely wonderful in here?"

Ewan agreed dutifully and went upstairs, where he waited in silence outside his bedroom. Then he seized the handle and flung the door open as if he could catch someone out.

The room was as he had left it. Nothing was out of place. A curtain moved, as if somebody had just shut the window.

Nothing more had happened by the time he went to bed, and he found he was disappointed. Perhaps this unhappy little girl would never slip into his time again. Mick, the dog, and the remote-controlled car were much more real than the child with the straggly red hair.

He woke suddenly, when the sun was still not fully up and the morning was gray, silent, and uncertain. He was thoroughly awake and clearheaded, knowing that he had slept deeply, without dreaming. He sat up.

Something had disturbed him. Something had happened in the room to wake him up. At the window opposite his bed, the curtain was moving.

He swung himself out of bed, pulled a sweater over his

pajamas, and padded in bare feet to the window. His bed was still his own; the familiar softness of the carpet was underfoot. The room was in his own time, but it was strangely quiet. It was as if somebody was hiding.

One swift swish, and he had opened the curtains. There was no trace of anyone. He took a good look behind them. Nothing.

The window was still shut. But there was an early-morning mist outside, and the window itself, rarely cleaned, had a mistiness of its own, which showed up a pattern so stark and clear that Ewan shivered. Across the haze on the glass, written very clearly in large, childish capitals, was:

HELP ME. ELSPETH.

Her face came vividly back to his mind, and the way she had reached out to him with fear and pleading in her eyes. Of course he would help her, if he could only find out what sort of help was needed.

He pushed his hands into the sleeves of his sweater for warmth and tried to think of what to do next. One thing seemed clear, from the sad and anxious face he had seen. Something had upset her and frightened her very badly.

He sat on his bed and wondered what she was afraid of. This must have been her room before it was his. He looked around at the furniture, which was his own, and the door, the closet, and the window frames, which had been there for so long. Every night he slept surrounded by the ancient stones of Ninian House with their histories of love and war, strength and defeat. In its moments of time change, it showed some of its past, but it must be crammed with other secrets that it never told. Whatever Elspeth was afraid of, it could still be there, in his room.

Ewan scowled a bit and told himself not to be stupid. He would have gone back to bed, but it didn't seem like a good idea anymore. Having already made the day's first great effort, which was getting up, it would be pointless to have to do it again. He crossed the landing, opened the opposite door, and found a room filled with neat heaps of stiff sheets, faded towels, and a smell of soap, warmth, and lavender. Typical. Just when he had gotten up early and gone for a wash without being told, the bathroom had turned into a Victorian linen cupboard again.

Ewan and Mick were the only people waiting for the bus outside the Loch Treen Post Office that morning. It was a shop as well as a post office—the only one Loch Treen had—and from there it was a fifteen-minute journey to school. The September day was chilly, with dampness in the air.

"Mum's looking for a long winter tenant for the cottage," said Mick. "It'll be bad news for the snooker table."

"Sorry, what did you say?" asked Ewan, who was thinking of Elspeth.

"The holiday cottage. She wants someone to rent it for the whole of the winter. She says we could do with the money, and we could, but I doubt she'll get anyone. Who'd want to come here in the winter?"

"Mick," said Ewan, "you know your gran? I mean, your great-gran?"

"Granny Carmichael? What about her?"

"She still remembers things that happened here a long way back, doesn't she?"

Mick shrugged. He took a pebble out of his pocket and inspected it, turning it over in his fingers.

"She's a wee bit scatty. She never knows whether she's taken her heart pills or whatever. But she's a walking history lesson, right enough. Oh, you're not telling me we're doing another wartime project, are we? I had to do that last year."

Ewan looked along the road to see if the school bus was coming. There were some things he didn't want to discuss in front of other people.

"Will you ask her if she knows anything about a family who lived in our house, say, between the wars? Ask her if she can remember a girl called Elspeth."

"Elspeth who?"

"Just Elspeth," he said as the bus drew into sight. "And will you ask her," he added more quietly, "if anything, you know, happened in our house?"

"What sort of anything?"

"You know." Ewan frowned. "Anything."

The bus was nearly there. The tiny phrase slipped out with quiet embarrassment. "Anything bad," he said.

Coming home that day, Ewan thought for a moment that the house had slipped into the future instead of the past. A wild shape of wrought iron and wheels stood in the hall, and green-and-silver metallic curtains hung over chairs and dangled from the banisters. But then his father emerged from the middle of the wrought iron, and his mother ran downstairs with an overflowing heap of green-and-purple drapery.

"What do you think?" asked his father, climbing out of the sculpture. "It's about industry and a sense of direction."

"The drapes are for the Glenfarden Hotel," said his mother. "They're planning a glitzy party, but it's not the color I ordered. I showed the suppliers exactly what I wanted. I was thinking seaweed. I told them, *Think seaweed.*"

Ewan was investigating the sculpture. "That's the only wheel off our barrow," he said, and ran upstairs. His bedroom was disappointingly normal as he changed out of his school uniform, but he did take a close look at the window in case there was anything new written there.

"I'm here," said a voice.

Ewan jumped. There was a cold prickling at the back of his neck, even though he recognized the child's voice with the soft Scots accent. Turning sharply he looked up, down, and around, but saw nobody.

"You can't see me," said the child. "It's awful hard work, to be seen and heard both at the same time. I can't manage it for long."

Ewan sat down on the bed and pretended he was just sitting there because he felt like it and not because his knees had gone weak. Time changes didn't usually scare him, but this was different. He stammered a bit before finding his voice.

"What do you want? What sort of help are you asking for?"

"I'm stuck," she said simply. "My name's Elspeth, and I'm nine years old. I've been around for years and years, but I'm still nine, and I'm still here."

"Are you . . . um . . ." It didn't seem polite to ask if she was dead, or a ghost, and he didn't want to upset her. "Are you—I mean, if you don't mind me asking, did you die here?"

There was a little sigh. "Sort of," she said. "That's the trouble."

"Sort of?" Ewan turned in the direction of the voice, which was somewhere between himself and the window. "How can you sort of die?"

"I didn't get the chance to finish it off properly," she said, and this time she sounded a touch irritated. "It wasn't my fault. I'll try to explain. It isn't easy. But you will listen, won't you?"

"Sure," said Ewan. "Shoot—I mean, go ahead."

- 3 -

I used to stay in this house," she said. "This was my bedroom, but not for very long. I caught diphtheria. That was in 1937, if you're particular about details. I was very ill, and I was dying."

"Oh, then you weren't . . ." interrupted Ewan, then said, "Sorry. Go on." But it was a relief to know that she had died of something normal, like an illness.

"This isn't easy," she said, rather huffily. "Do you want to know or not?"

"Sorry," said Ewan again.

"Just as I died," she continued, "the house did a time shift. It went medieval all around me, you know, the way it sometimes does."

"Yes, I know."

"So I was in the wrong time. You can't die, not completely, not properly, if you're in the wrong time. And when I got back to my right time, my own time, I'd missed my moment and got stuck."

Ewan tried to work this out but couldn't.

"But then you wouldn't be dead," he said. "You would still have been breathing."

"No, I was not," she said firmly.

"But you must have been," argued Ewan, struggling to understand this. The lampshade suddenly rocked above him, and the light flickered on and off.

"Sorry," snapped Elspeth. "I didn't mean to do that, but things happen when I get annoyed. What do you know about dying, if you're so clever? You've never died, have you?"

"Well, no, I haven't. I'm sorry, this is hard to understand."

"And I suppose you think death is a simple thing, do you?" she went on scathingly. "One second you're alive, then your body switches off and you're dead. That's what you think, isn't it?"

Ewan felt he'd had enough of being lectured at. "If you're going to be snippy, I won't help you," he said. "This is my room now, and however long you've been here, if you're still nine, you're younger than I am."

There was a silence. He wondered if she'd gone away in a huff, or if he'd scared her.

"Sorry," said a small and very unhappy voice at last.

"All right, go on. But don't go all bossy again, or I won't listen."

"I *was* dead, in the way that you mean it," she said, much more calmly, as if she was afraid of annoying him again. "My heart wasn't beating, and I'd stopped breathing, so, yes, I was dead. But I hadn't got through to where I should be." Her voice softened with sorrow and longing. "I needed to go into the music. That's where I should have gone. I should be there now. I wanted it so much."

Ewan didn't know what "the music" was, but it must be something wonderful. From the yearning in her voice, Elspeth was breaking her heart to be there.

"I don't understand," he said. "What music?"

"The singing," she explained, which didn't help much. "It's . . . it's light. Rainbows. A party. All the love. Singing, but not like our sort of singing. Och, you know."

"Do you mean heaven?" asked Ewan, who had never been quite sure if he believed in it.

"I suppose that's what you'd call it. But when you've seen just a wee glimmer of it, 'heaven' isn't enough. I should be there, but my journey was interrupted, you see, when the house did that funny thing that it does, and I missed my moment. And ever since then, I've not been able to get there." Her voice grew fainter, so that Ewan had to listen hard. "I've tried, but I can't."

"So what do you want me to do?" Ewan looked around. It was unsettling, hearing the voice and not seeing her. He could imagine the pale face, framed by red hair, but he couldn't see it. "Do you want me to help you get there? If I can, I will. What do I have to do?"

There was no answer.

"Elspeth?" he called. "Are you there?"

She must be there. She'd just told him she'd been trapped in there ever since 1937, but he couldn't hear her anymore.

He waited. Then he unpacked his schoolbag and sorted out his homework to take it downstairs, because the log fire had been lit in the sitting room. That fire was one of the great treats of Ninian House. At his bedroom door, he turned and looked around once more.

"Elspeth?" he said.

There was a whisper, as slight as a feather in the air.

"Too tired. Later."

Ewan's father was on his knees on the living room floor, hunting through the basket of logs. Bits of a dismantled sculpture and a wooden crate lay beside him.

"All this wood, and none of it exactly right," he said. "I was going to use that crate for a framework, but it's no good. It can go on the fire."

"Don't!" Ewan, who had been looking for something like this, pounced on the crate. "Can I have it? There's not enough space in my desk for my schoolbooks."

"'Course you can." Ewan's father dusted himself down and rubbed his sooty hands on his jeans before picking up Ewan's homework notebook. "But I didn't think you were short of storage space. You've got one of those big wall closets in there, haven't you?"

The closets in Ninian House were really useful—or, at least, the ones that opened were. They had been built into the thickness of the massive stone walls, and they had wooden doors stained dark with age. Some of those closets could be used, but some were jammed or had been locked years ago with long-lost keys. Ewan's was completely solid. He had given up heaving against it and jiggling the doorknob and trying out different keys and had put the poster over it instead.

"My closet won't open and my wardrobe's full," he said. He rescued the crate and ran upstairs with it before his father could change his mind.

"Elspeth?" he said, but there was still no sound. He took the crate to the other side of the bed, intending to put it down in front of the closet, but some uneasy feeling, like an instinct, told him it didn't belong there. He left it by the desk instead. That was where everything ended up— sports stuff, games, toys that were not quite outgrown, and the clothes he couldn't be bothered to put in his wardrobe. Cluttered as it was, he put the crate there, too, because he felt that was where it should be.

Was it because of Elspeth? Did she want it there, and not anywhere near the closet? Ewan considered this for a minute, then decided it was ridiculous.

He went downstairs again and found his father earnestly reading his homework diary, and from the bright keenness on his face, something was making him happy. He turned his eager smile on Ewan.

"You've got art homework!" he announced happily.

"It's just a sketch," said Ewan quickly. "And it's for an assignment, so we're not allowed to have help with it."

"Oh," Ewan's father said, visibly disappointed. Dad loved helping with art homework. Unfortunately he tended to take over, and his idea of art homework usually ended up as something three-dimensional and made from the insides of an old washing machine. It would always be too big to get on the school bus, and nothing to do with the work that was assigned in the first place.

He spread his books over the table and bent his head over them, hoping his father would stop hovering and think of something to do in the cellar, which had become his studio.

His father glanced over his shoulder. "Is that a graph?"

"Yes, it's nearly finished," Ewan said, and bent his head even closer with an air of concentration. Not knowing what his parents would do next could be a problem, but sometimes knowing was worse.

"Couldn't you do it three-dimensionally?"

"No," said Ewan firmly. "We're not allowed to." But he felt a little sorry for his father as he clumped down to the cellar. Sometimes he wondered if all fathers were like that—forgetting everything except work for hours at a time, then trying too hard to make up for it and be a Really Good Father. It was always one extreme or the other.

He settled down to work and continued until a car door slammed and his mother swished into the house with a click-clack of sharp heels. The room flickered and changed. It was bare, candlelit, and a bit drafty, with a stale and smoky smell. There were rushes on the floor, and an enormous dog lay on its side, beating its tail in contentment. An old man with a stooped back carried in a gigantic basket of logs.

"Oh," said his mother from the doorway, "we've gone medieval."

The scene disappeared. The room was bright and warm and furnished again.

"Very picturesque," she said. "And I love those natural color tones. But I wouldn't like to stay in the Middle Ages for long."

"I suppose it would be all right if you didn't know about anything else," said Ewan. "I mean, if you'd never heard of things like, say, cars and computers . . ."

"Yes, and central heating, pizza, and aspirin," put in his mother.

"You wouldn't miss them. But it must be terrible to get stuck in the wrong time."

"Horrible," she said. "Speaking of pizza, there's some in the freezer." And she click-clacked away.

After dinner, Ewan went upstairs to get his jacket before going over to Mick's. He waited to see if his room would change again, or if Elspeth would appear. He was about to give up when he remembered the window.

He could still see her name. Underneath it, she had

added "Cooper." The letters sloped downwards toward the right as if the writer was growing tired.

"Cooper? Och, no, son, there was never any Cooper." Granny Carmichael, Mick's great-gran, put her head a little to one side and spoke with absolute confidence. She was very small and thin-boned, and her fingers were crooked at the knuckles. In spite of her great age she never wore glasses, always looking and listening with great attention, tilting her head toward the speaker. To Ewan, she seemed like a white-haired robin.

"There was the Urquharts had Ninian House, many years," she said. "And then it was left empty, then the Sutherlands took it. Then an English family called Brook, or Brookes, or something, they had it, then the Scotts, but mind, they never settled. They soon flitted. Then it was empty until yourselves moved in."

"But I was sure there was a little girl there," said Ewan, "in 1937. Somebody was telling me."

"Thirty-seven?" The crinkles of Granny Carmichael's face deepened as she frowned with thought. "No, laddie, it was the Sutherlands that had it then. I remember them, though I was away working in Dumfries by then, so I never saw them so often. There were three sons, and they were all A's: Alan, Adam, and Alexander. An awful daft idea, if you ask me. Never a lassie in that family. Who's been telling you this?"

Ewan looked down to avoid the sharpness of those bright eyes. "I'm not sure who it was."

"Well, whoever it was, they must be away with the fairies. You could have a wee word with Mrs. Craigie, though."

"Mrs. Craigie in the post office?" said Ewan, unconvinced.

Granny Carmichael gave a mischievous chuckle that seemed to belong to somebody much younger. "She's no' as ancient as I am! Aye, but she's been many a year in that shop, and she knows all the old stories as well as the new ones. The oldies all stand around and tell her their life stories, and their mothers' and fathers' life stories, too, as if they'd nothing to do and all day to do it in. Now, d'you think I've earned a turn with the wee car, Ewan? You'll have to remind me what to do."

That was another great thing about Mick's Granny Carmichael. She didn't turn up her nose in scorn at modern toys and say that young people have no imagination. She loved the remote-controlled car, but her hands were just a bit shaky, so Ewan had to help her.

"We never had these when I was a lassie," she said as the car hit the wall and turned on its roof. "We'd have loved them. We'd never have done any work on the farm all day, never the milking, nor the egg washing, if we'd had playthings like these."

Ewan, Mick, and Gran took turns with the remote-controlled car until it was time for Ewan to go. Cycling home to Ninian House, he saw a flood of yellow light from the front door.

His father was in the doorway. He walked slowly toward the loch, a pale flashlight beam bobbing and weaving in his hand, as Ewan's bike slowed and grumbled over the gravel, and his father swung the light to look at him.

"Were you looking for me, Dad? I phoned to say when I'd be back."

"No, no," he said airily, and Ewan knew that it had been a silly question, because his father didn't have a clue about things like that. Mum was the fussy one. "I came out to do some real thinking. Isn't it a beautiful night?"

It was. It was dark and clear, and the autumn frosts had not started. There were no streetlights here, only the glow from Ninian House and the scattered lights of far-off cottages. A halo shone around the flashlight and around the lights on Ewan's bike. The moon glowed softly in the sky and in the loch, rippling calmly. A fox barked.

"Do you know," said his father slowly, "all the work I've done for the last six months has been a load of rubbish."

Ewan wasn't sure if he should agree. "Has it?" he said.

"And do you know why it's been a load of rubbish? Because I haven't seen what's in front of my nose. I've been doing exactly the sort of work I've done for years, and here I am"—he turned around slowly—"here I am in the middle of all this . . . this . . . this *power,* and I'm ignoring it. I should be drawing on this. I should be using moss and lichens and natural materials. Natural colors. I should be looking at living creatures. I should try to show the earthiness, the life. What sort of creature—I mean, what sort of animal—does this place make you think of, Ewan?"

Ewan hugged himself for warmth. "I like the red squirrels," he said. "And there's the foxes. Pheasants." He glanced up at his father's face and saw that nothing was registering. He thought again and had a spark of inspiration. "Eagles."

"Eagles." His father seemed to like this. "Eagles . . . No, bigger than eagles. Stronger than eagles." Then he threw open his arms as if he wanted to declare love for all Loch Treen and for all the world. "I need a lion! A *lion!*"

It was still cold. Ewan decided that this was not the best time to point out that lions weren't typical of Loch Treen. He wheeled his bike around to put it away and saw, through the open front door, a square of patterned brown carpet and a hat stand. He looked up.

The light at his window was dim—it might have been candle or lamp light. Whatever it was, it showed him Elspeth.

H e ran for the stairs, but before he was halfway up, the house had returned to its own year. In a wild hope that Elspeth might still be visible, he made a dash for the bedroom door and threw it open.

It was Elspeth's room, with her patchwork quilt and her rug on the floor. Elspeth, in her nightdress, was at the window.

"The past has stayed longer in here," said Ewan.

"That's because I'm here," said Elspeth. "It's fitting itself in with me." There was a flicker that made Ewan blink, and the room was his own again. "It's fitting in with you now," she explained. And she faded, slowly, as he watched her.

"Elspeth, I've only just found you!" he cried. "Are you still there? How can I talk to you if we're not in the same time and place?"

"Of course I'm still here." She sounded annoyed, and

the light flickered. "I'm always here, more's the pity. Where else could I be?"

"No need to get snappy again," said Ewan. "Elspeth, I've just been talking to my friend's gran, and she said—"

"Oh, never mind what she said. This is urgent, Ewan. I don't know how long I can talk to you without wearing myself thin, so you'll have to listen while I'm still able to talk. What I've been doing, over all these years since I died, is waiting for the right time change. I need to get back to the moment when I was dying. I died on the twenty-fifth of October 1937, at nine minutes past eleven at night. When the house slips back to that moment and shows it again, I should be able to get through—go back to my dying, and do it properly."

"But the chances of that are . . ." He thought of all the seconds that had passed since an October day in 1937 and didn't even attempt to work it out. "Impossible!"

"But it does come round again!" she insisted, and her voice became high and rapid. "Sometimes the date does come back. It was an important moment, so the house comes back to it. I've been there before, but . . ."

There was a pause and a bit of a sniff. Ewan wanted to give her a tissue, then realized he couldn't.

"Sorry," continued Elspeth in a small voice. "Three times, the house has come back to that exact moment, and I've really, really thought I was going to slip into the singing. I could see the party, and hear it. I was all ready to be there! But it never works! It should, but it never does, and I don't know why. Every time I tried to get through, but I couldn't . . . I couldn't . . ."

The room transformed into Elspeth's room again, then back to Ewan's, then back to Elspeth's, flickering between the two as if someone were changing TV channels very quickly. Ewan waited for it to stop, but it repeated over and over again, faster and faster, making him squint dizzily against it.

"If you're making that happen, Elspeth, will you stop it!"

"I'm sorry, I don't mean to. It happens when I get into a stooshie."

"A what?"

"How long have you been in Scotland, and you don't know what a stooshie is? A state. Agitated. All of a whatnot. That's a stooshie. I'm better now, and I'll try to tell you this very gently so the room doesn't shake anymore. I'd hate to scare you."

Ewan picked up the teasing note in the soft Scots voice.

"I'm not scared. It's just annoying. So why couldn't you get through to the singing?"

"Something was in the way. Something hard. I could almost touch it. But I think if I had somebody here with me, I could get through."

"Oh, I see. You mean me?"

There was a pause, then she asked shyly, "Would you? Please?"

"What would I have to do?" he asked. "I mean, I wouldn't have to go with you, would I?"

"Of course not! It isn't your time. The most important thing is that you don't do anything."

"But I thought you said—"

"No, you mustn't *do* anything. You've no idea the trouble it causes when know-it-alls and busybodies try to *do* something about people like me. If there was a nice priest who really understood what was happening, that might be different. Somebody who's good at opening doors, like a kind of peterman."

There was almost a smile in her voice, as if she had said something funny. Ewan wanted to ask her what a peterman was, but she went on, "All you need to do is to be there. Just be there, and care enough to want me to be free. Can you do that?"

"Sure." It sounded easy enough. "When will it be?"

"Soon. I don't know precisely, but I can feel it."

"What if your moment comes, and I'm not here?"

"That's a chance we have to take. It's always been an evening or a night time, up to now."

"If I'm asleep, you'll have to wake me."

Elspeth giggled. "Of course I will. I'm always here. I never sleep. Even if you leave the door open, I'm locked in here and I can't get out."

Something new occurred to Ewan, and he didn't like it. "When I can't see you, which is most of the time," he said, "can you see me?"

She giggled again. "Och, yes! Of course I can!"

He'd been afraid she'd say that. He tried not to look too

conspicuously at the football boots on the floor, the scatter of dirty laundry, the candy wrappers that had missed the wastepaper basket, the rather childish toys that he hadn't felt able to part with.

"So what?" she said. "Do you think I care? There's nothing in here to get fashed about."

"That's not the point," said Ewan. He'd already decided to get changed in the bathroom in the future. Even if it slipped back five hundred years and wasn't a bathroom anymore, it was better than being watched by a girl.

Mick understood that. Ewan told him about it as they came home on the school bus the next day, talking in low voices and sitting apart from the others.

"She's there all the time," he said. "It's not that I have anything against her, but it's not right. My own room isn't my own at all."

"But she doesn't do any harm, does she?"

"That's not the point. How would you like to have someone watching you all the time?"

Mick was used to the grinning faces of his little sisters appearing around the bedroom door at embarrassing moments. He nodded in sympathy.

"The trouble is, she was there long before I knew about her," said Ewan. "So for all that time . . ."

Mick tried not to smile, but couldn't help it.

"Oh, shut up, Mick," said Ewan.

"Didn't say a word," said Mick, fighting the grin on his

face. The bus had reached Loch Treen by now. They hoisted their schoolbags onto their shoulders and clumped down the stairs of the bus. A spiteful little cold wind spat drizzle into their faces and fussed at the surface of the loch, and as if by telepathy they both turned for the post office.

Mrs. Craigie, small, neat, and fidgety, sat at the counter. They bought some of the crumbly homemade sweet that Ewan called fudge and everybody else called tablet, and Ewan asked, "Mrs. Craigie, do you know anything about some people who used to live in our house before the war? Granny Carmichael thought you might know."

Mrs. Craigie seemed to find this very funny and gave a squeaky little laugh.

"I don't go back so far as Mick's great-granny! It's a long way before my time!"

"But she says you know all the old stories," said Mick.

"That they've been handed down to you," added Ewan.

"Well, then," she said, and Ewan supposed she liked to think of herself as the keeper of Loch Treen's past. "What do you want to know?"

"There was a family at Ninian House in the thirties," said Ewan. "The Sutherlands. They had three sons."

"All A's." Mrs. Craigie fidgeted with her necklace. "All lads, no lassies."

"But somebody said to me that there was a little girl who lived there, and it must have been about that time. Her name was Elspeth Cooper."

Mrs. Craigie let go of the necklace and looked past him with such concentration that she seemed to go into a trance. Finally, she said, "No. I've never heard of an Elspeth Cooper, or Elspeth anyone at that house. She must have stayed somewhere else."

"No, it was definitely Ninian House."

"I'm sorry. I can't help you."

Ewan looked helplessly at Mick, and Mick shrugged. They turned to go. There was nothing else to do. The bell jangled as Mick opened the door, and the cold filtered in.

"Och!" called Mrs. Craigie. "Yes, of course! I know who you mean!"

- 5 -

They let the door bang noisily. Ewan, feeling the color rise in his face, hurried back to the counter.

"You mean the little cousin," said Mrs. Craigie. "I know very little about her. Mrs. Sutherland had a sister, and the sister's husband was something in the civil service—he worked abroad somewhere. Was it India? Aye, I recall it may have been India.

"It's an awful sad story. They were going back to India, and it didn't suit them to take the little lassie with them. She was sent to live with her aunt and uncle in that big, lonely house. There were the boys, but they were older than she was and all away at boarding school. And the poor wee thing caught diphtheria and died. You've no idea what it was like in those days, before they had vaccinations and antibiotics. So she never saw her own mum and daddy again. I'm not sure what age she would have been, but she was younger than the boys. Is that any use to you?"

"It's exactly what I needed to know. Thanks, Mrs.

Craigie," said Ewan. He bought two bags of potato chips out of gratitude. He gave one to Mick, and they ate as they walked home. They had to hold the bags close to them as the rain grew heavier.

"What Mrs. Craigie said didn't make much difference," said Mick. "You already knew Elspeth was there, and what she died of."

"But I know more now," said Ewan. "And it makes her a lot more real. She has a place in the world."

"Not just in your bedroom," added Mick, and, as they were both hunched against the wind and rain, Ewan couldn't see if he was smiling.

"Come away in, Ewan," called Mick's mum when they reached the cottage. "You don't want to walk home in this. Phone home, let them know where you are. Stop and have your supper with us."

It was no good phoning home. Dad would be up to his eyes in the moss, rocks, and rolls of chicken wire he was now using to make a lion. Ewan called his mother on her cell phone as Mick's little sisters peeped around the door and pressed both hands to their mouths to squash the giggles.

"I don't know what time I'll be back," she said, her voice buzzing and fading over the line. "I'll pick you up from Mick's on my way home."

"Haven't you any idea when?"

"None at all. Sorry. See you later."

Ewan put the phone down and bent to make a fuss over Bruce, who could knock him over just by rubbing against his legs. Then he went to join Mick in Granny Carmichael's room. Mick always took her a cup of tea when he came in from school, and she always gave him a toffee. She almost lived on tea and toffees.

"Mick was telling me you've found out about the wee girl," she said, throwing him a wrapped sweet.

"Yes, Mrs. Craigie told us," said Ewan.

"I remember her now," she said rather thickly, her mouth full. "I saw her once in the kirk." She shuffled the toffee into her cheek and went on. "I was away in Dumfries, working as a housemaid, but I came home for a wee while and heard that Mr. and Mrs. Sutherland had their niece staying. Her parents didn't want her, and I'm no' sure the Sutherlands did, either, but they took her in. They were all in the kirk that morning, all those tall laddies in their Sunday suits and this wispy little red-haired bairn. She looked as if she'd been picked up and dropped in the wrong picture, like a flower at a leek show." She gave a little *hmph!* of laughter at the thought. Then her face saddened. "I heard she died of the diphtheria, poor lamb. There were many who did, in those days. It can't have been much of a life for her, in that big house with just her uncle and aunt."

Mick's mum looked around the door.

"The good news, lads, is that I've put the snooker table in the holiday cottage for you."

"Great!" They both jumped to their feet.

"The bad news is, it's lying with its top against one wall and its legs against another. You'll have to put it together yourselves."

They ran out into the rain. By now, it was a real Scots storm crashing across the loch.

"Come in if the power goes off!" yelled Mick's mum. Ewan, under the bright electric lights, looked up.

"Is it likely to go off?"

Mick shrugged. "We sometimes get power cuts in this weather. We'll turn the table on its back to screw the legs in."

They set to work quickly, knowing that they'd have to hurry if they were to get much of a game in before supper. The table was up and they had played half a frame when they were called back to the house to work their way through heaped plates of sausages and potatoes, followed by lemon cake. After all that, Ewan's mum had still not arrived.

"Finish the game?" said Mick.

"Sure," said Ewan.

"Oh, and Ewan," called Mick's mum after him, "be sure to tell your mother that if we do have any power cuts, she can bring anything from her freezer and put it into mine. We can run everything off the genny in emergencies."

"The what?" asked Ewan.

"The generator, you hopeless Englishman," said Mick. "Are you coming to play this game out?"

"I'm not an Englishman," said Ewan.

"You're not a Scot."

"I'm a Borderer. It's your turn."

They played, and Ewan might have won, but his concentration failed. Uneasiness was spreading through him. All the time, as he surveyed the table, as he took aim with the cue stick and scattered the colored balls, it was as if a voice was calling him. As if a child tugged at his sweater, more and more insistently, telling him, *You have to go home.*

It was not someone else's voice. It was his own voice, a voice he felt rather than heard, from deep inside him, urging him.

I need to go home.

Angle the shot. Pocket the red. Now go for the yellow.

I need to go home.

Yellow. Missed it. Watch what Mick does.

I need to go home.

Blue. Can't hit it from here. Walk around the table. I think I know how to do this.

I need to go NOW. NOW.

Thwack, smack, roll, and drop into the pocket. Good. Ewan straightened up, the cue still in his hand.

"I need to go home," he said quickly.

"But we haven't finished!" objected Mick. "And your mum's not here!"

"I can go without her. I'm not an infant."

The need to be home tore at him, but he could see Mick's hurt and indignation at the idea of missing out on the game. So they played it out, but Ewan no longer cared whether he won or lost. All he wanted was to end it quickly.

The balls clacked and scurried into the pockets, and Ewan lost. They shook hands.

"Good win," said Ewan.

"I wouldn't have won," said Mick, "if you'd played your best. Are you going home now? You're daft! The rain's coming down in stair rods, and that wind would blow the hair off a nanny goat! Wait for your mum!"

"She could be ages yet. You know what she's like."

"Wear my waterproofs, then."

They darted through the tearing rain back to the house. In the hall, Ewan pulled on Mick's raincoat.

"Oh, is she here, then?" called Mick's mother.

"I just have to go," blurted Ewan.

"Flashlight." Mick pushed one into his hand, and already Ewan was halfway out to the gate, running hard toward the distant lights of Ninian House.

The total darkness took him by surprise. He had forgotten the thick, black stretch of night in a place with no street lighting, and the flashlight beam was only enough to cast a dimly shaking circle on the few feet in front of him. He looked over his shoulder at the warmly lit windows of Mick's cottage. It was already farther away, but as he ran, Ninian House looked no nearer.

The glance over his shoulder had shown him another light. One that appeared and disappeared again.

Of course, he told himself, it's only the lights from Mum's car. But there was no point in stopping and waiting in the rain for her to catch up, and the call of Ninian

House was irresistible. He glanced around once more as he ran, tripped on a stone, stumbled, stepped deep in a puddle, and ran on with water squelching cold in his shoes. The flashlight showed him raindrops pelting into a lake of puddle water, and he swerved to avoid it, tripped again, and ran into the branches of a tree. A merciless chilling of raindrops slipped between his collar and the back of his neck. Slithering, he stumbled back to the path—or to where he thought the path should be.

There was no path. He cast about with the flashlight, which seemed fainter than it had been. He slipped in mud and slid onto his back. After he'd picked himself up, he tried to work out where he was.

"The car lights should be over there," he told himself, "but they're not. She must have parked and turned them off." The flashlight was now nothing but a pinprick of poor yellow light. He looked for Ninian House, but it seemed that there was no Ninian House.

For the first time in his life, Ewan knew absolute darkness. Darkness and abandonment. He had no sense of where he would be with the next step. He could walk into the road or into the heather, into the broken rocks at the side of the loch or into the loch itself. He inched forward, feeling with one shuffling foot at a time as the rain lashed against him, trickling down his face, dripping from his nose and his hair, seeping through his shoes. Squinting over his shoulder through the rain, he could see lights on at Mick's house. Why hadn't he seen them before? And what had happened to Ninian House? Had it gone into a time change, back to an age with no electricity, at the worst possible moment?

The need to be there, the tug of urgency that had called him away from the safety of Mick's warm cottage, was mixed now with desperation to be home for his own sake. With his head down, he struggled forward against the storm, fighting for every step. He would never be there again, never dry, never again see daylight; he would be locked forever in drenching darkness, not knowing where the sky ended and the loch began. He took a step and plunged knee-deep into cold water. Gasping and slipping, his hands pained with cold, he scrambled out as the car engine roared nearer and the headlights loomed and shone.

Click-bang went the door. The sudden flood of light from the car and the sight of his mother, brightly dressed, her face sharp with worry, startled him as if he had walked into another world.

"What do you think you're doing! Get in the car! Why did you run away from Mick's like that?"

He tried to speak as he stumbled into the car, but he was too cold to frame the words, and it didn't matter. It didn't matter how cross she was, either. The world had been transformed and become safe.

"You're soaked through," she snapped.

Ewan struggled to speak clearly. "Just had to get home,"

he stammered through the numbing cold. "Had to." He made one more effort. "You were late."

"That's the way it is sometimes," she said, a little less sharply. She glanced at him. "Sorry."

"Watch the road, Mum," he said.

"The power's off," she said, after an uneasy pause.

"Mick's mum says you can use—"

"The freezer, yes," she said. She parked the car outside Ninian House, a rough gray crag against the heavy sky. "Get straight in the bath. It's the only way you'll get warm."

They dashed for the front door, and she searched with her fingers for the lock before they could stumble indoors. A single candle stuck in a saucer made the hall so dismal it might have been in some miserable Dark Age winter for all anyone could tell. His mother swept into the kitchen, saying something about getting the wood-burning stove going, but Ewan's father was already there, and the brightness of the growing flames in the dark drew Ewan toward it like an enchantment.

"Beautiful wood grain," his father said with reverence. "Seems a shame to burn it."

"For pity's sake, Simon, shove it on the fire."

Ewan's mother pushed three or four logs into the stove, banged the door shut, and turned up the draft to fan the flames. "Don't stand there, Ewan! Candles and matches in the dresser. Run yourself a bath."

He left his wet shoes and socks in the kitchen and didn't wait to find a candle. Still shivering, and feeling his way up the stairs, he banged the flashlight on the stone wall, and it flickered obediently back to life.

He opened his bedroom door. "Elspeth?" His teeth chattered, and it was hard to speak. "Are you there? Are you all right?"

"'Course I'm all right," came Elspeth's voice. She sounded very calm and dreamy. She might almost have been happy.

He curled up on the floor, still shivering, and rubbed life into his cold feet. "I ran back in the storm. I had to get back. I thought something was wrong."

"No," said Elspeth in a faraway voice.

Nothing to worry about there, then. He'd be better off soaking in a hot bath than exchanging small talk with Elspeth, who didn't seem to care whether he was there or not, let alone what he'd gone through to get home in case she needed him. He grabbed some dry clothes from the heap on the floor and took himself off to the bathroom.

The bath was worth getting cold and wet for. He set candles on the windowsill and lay back in the hot water as the chill seeped out and the heat soaked in, steady and strong, through every layer of skin and every vein to the core of his bones. Rising steam lifted across the candle flames, misty mysterious in the dark. He filled the tub to the brim and washed his hair. As he came out of the bathroom, the lights flickered back on.

"Thank goodness for that," said his mother, who was running up the stairs with a candle in her hand. She still sounded cross. "I was just about to take the freezer stuff down the road. I phoned Mick's mum—she was worried about you. So was I. I thought you'd fallen in the loch."

"I did."

"You *did?*"

For a moment, Ewan thought she might hit him.

"Don't you ever," she warned in a grim, quiet voice, "*ever* scare me like that again." It was safest not to answer, and he escaped to his own room.

"That was your mother I could hear talking, wasn't it," said Elspeth in her new, dreamy way. "She's really nice."

"Nice!" Ewan flopped on to his bed.

"You should have met mine," she went on. "She wouldn't have cared if I fell in the loch. Not that it matters now."

"Elspeth, tell me what's going on," Ewan insisted. "And don't go all airy-fairy and tell me it's all right. One minute I was playing snooker with Mick and beating him off the face of the earth, and then I had to come back. I couldn't help it, even though the rain was coming down in bucketloads. When the power went off, there was a moment when I felt like I'd never get home again. It was as if something was trying to stop me."

"Don't be silly," said Elspeth, suddenly sounding snappy and annoyed. "You got here, didn't you?"

"Yes, I got here and found you talking like a fairy-tale princess mooning over a frog. I bet if I could see you, you'd be gazing out that window."

There was a giggle from the direction of the window.

"You can't even see out at this time of night," he pointed out.

"It's different for me," she said. There was a rising note of excitement in her voice, which was quicker but quiet again. "I didn't send for you. I can't do that. But you were right, you do need to be here. The music feels so close, I can almost touch it. Haven't you felt it, too? I know it. It'll be tonight."

He heard the intensity of tightly held joy in her voice, as if she could burst with hope before the moment came. "Very soon now. You'll be with me, won't you, Ewan? You'll help me break through?"

"I'll be here," he said.

- 6 -

When he woke, he was already sitting up in darkness with a feeling of tight excitement. It was as if a taut string had been plucked or a chord struck, and the vibrations were still quivering, holding on, holding, not wanting to fade. He swung out of bed, reached for his sweater, and, standing, felt not the carpet but the cold floor under his feet.

The dim glow in the room came from an oil lamp, and the lamp stood on a wooden table by the bed with the patchwork cover. He had just gotten out of his own bed, but the one he was looking at now was Elspeth's. She lay, her eyes closed, under a rumpled white sheet, and it hurt Ewan to look at her.

An armchair had been pulled to the side of the bed, close enough for the tall woman sitting there to reach out and touch Elspeth, but she had fallen asleep, slumped in the chair. Her hair was short, wavy, and graying, and though it was night, she was fully clothed, with a blanket wrapped around her for warmth. On the table at her elbow was a half-empty glass of some sort of fruit drink, a jug, and a teacup and saucer. There was something in a long, thin case that Ewan guessed might be a thermometer. A fountain pen lay there, too, with its cap off, and a sheet of notepaper had fallen on the floor, as if the woman had been writing a letter before she fell asleep.

Ewan made himself look at Elspeth. Even if he didn't, he could hear her struggle to breathe, as if every breath was such a fight that it would be too hard to finish. He took in her thin face, her damp hair, and her dry, cracked lips. The woman in the chair slowly raised her head, opened her eyes with a heavy effort, and, struggling against sleep, sat up and leaned over to look closely at Elspeth.

There was a silence so frightening that it seemed to last for years.

Elspeth did not take the next breath.

The woman leaned over her, calling her name. She called again, urgent and anxious. She took Elspeth's thin wrist in her hand and felt for a pulse.

Elspeth's familiar voice in his ear startled him. He jumped.

"Open the window," she said. He ran across the floor and opened it.

"Good-bye, Ewan," she whispered. "I'm sorry if I've been a bit nattery sometimes. And thanks."

What happened next was something Ewan could not see or touch or hear, but it was very real. There was a disturbance all around him, as if a flock of birds were about to rise into the air, or a door about to fly open, or a ship about to be launched. It gathered strength and direction, and a rush of movement swept toward the window. Whatever it was, this power and this moment of flight, it poured past him as it surged forward.

Then it stopped. He could feel it slam to a stop, like a bird hitting a window. But Elspeth's window was open; nothing was in the way—he even put his hand out, to make sure that he felt the air, not glass. The movement gathered and surged forward again, and again it stopped.

"Come on, Elspeth," he whispered. "You can go! Come on, get out before it's too late!"

The room changed from Elspeth's time to his, then back, faster and faster. Then it appeared as a medieval chamber, then as Elspeth's room again, then modern, then Victorian, then Elspeth's, flicking and changing so fast that Ewan's balance failed, and he fell to the floor. Around him the surging went on, beating against the window—but it was weaker now, fading, and as the room flashed from Elspeth's time to his own, it failed completely. He was in his own room, in the dark, with the sound of a child sobbing.

He picked himself up and staggered to the light switch. By the window, Elspeth sat curled on the floor, shuddering with sobs too terrible to be borne. She raised her blotchy, tear-stained face and drew her sleeve across her eyes.

"I couldn't do it." She gulped and fought to speak through tears. "I'm still here."

It had grown very cold in the night. Ewan plugged in

the electric heater and sat on the floor beside Elspeth, pulling his sweater over his knees. He put his arm around her, then realized that he couldn't put an arm around someone who wasn't really there—but he felt as if *something* was there, and his hand didn't just pass through her thin shoulders. She leaned against him, still crying.

"I'm here forever," she sobbed, struggling to manage the words.

"You're not. There'll be another time. Was it me, Elspeth? Did I do something wrong? If I did, I'm sorry."

"No," she sniffed. "It wasn't you. It's because of . . ."

"It's because of what?" She didn't answer, so he asked again. "It's *what,* Elspeth?"

"It's not because of anything," she said weakly, as if all the fight had been knocked out of her. She was looking at the floor, not at him.

Ewan studied her and said, "I don't believe you."

"Don't be so horrible," she whimpered.

"Then don't you be pathetic. Yes, I know you're disappointed, but there's no need to go all Poor Little Me about it and lie to me when I'm trying to help you. What did you mean by 'because of'? All I want is to go back to bed. After all that's happened tonight, I wouldn't be able to sleep, but at least I'd be warm."

"Go, then," she said, but as if she didn't really want him to.

"I'm staying here." He huddled his knees up tightly. "I'm staying until you tell me the truth. Something was stopping you from getting out tonight. I don't know what it was, but there was something there. If I'm going to help you, I need to know what we're up against."

"I'm too tired for this," said Elspeth, who really did look paler and fainter than before. Even so, Ewan wondered if she was making excuses.

"I'm not like you," he insisted. "I sleep in this room every night, and if there's something—something dangerous in here, I want to know about it. Has something terrible happened here?" She still didn't answer, and he had to go on asking questions, though it might be better not to know the answers. "Was there ever a murder here, Elspeth? Was somebody kept a prisoner?"

"No," she said, very softly. "None of that." She seemed paler all the time.

"Your aunt and uncle? Please, Elspeth, tell me. Were they cruel to you?"

"No," she whispered, but he was sure her resistance was weakening as she grew fainter. He could feel it.

"Well, what is it, then?" He hugged his knees even tighter. "I'm going to sit here till you tell me." He looked hard into her face, willing her to look at him, though by now she was almost transparent. "Please? *Please?*"

There was a long, sad sigh, and she was not there. Her last wisp of strength seemed to waft away on that sigh, and Ewan was left alone, in a sudden emptiness. But into the silence that followed, came the whisper of her voice.

"Alex," she said.

- 7 -

Waking in the morning, he knew that he had slept much later than usual. Then, with blissful satisfaction, he remembered that it was Saturday. As he rolled over and burrowed down into the warm quilt, he was aware that Elspeth had been upset and worn out last night. She might still be distressed and want his company, but his eyes wanted to close again, and stay closed. He sank into a dream in which his father was building a life-size model of Mrs. Craigie out of kettles and saucepans, and when it was nearly finished, it turned into Elspeth. Mick was in the dream, too, and was asking Elspeth if she was dead.

"I said, 'Are you dead, or can you roll yourself out of there?'" came Mick's voice. There was the clink of a dog's ID tag and a padding of paws.

Ewan sat up, rubbed his eyes, and put one arm around Bruce, who had both front paws on the bed and was trying to lick him.

"Get down, Bruce," ordered Mick. He sat on the floor

and pulled Bruce toward him. "Your dad said to come up. He thought you were hibernating."

Ewan pulled the quilt around him, as it was colder than usual.

"I was up half the night," he said, but already he doubted it. Mick was real and solid, cross-legged on the floor in his stockinged feet. Bruce, with his wagging tail and his smell of life and warm fur, was real. Ewan couldn't have stood here last night, and certainly not in 1937, comforting a heartbroken ghost in the dark. Perhaps he'd dreamed it.

"Do you always leave the window open all night?" said Mick. He walked to the window, with Bruce following, and shut it.

"It did happen," said Ewan, half to himself.

Picking up his clothes, he told Mick what had happened, then, aware of Elspeth's invisible presence, went to the bathroom to wash and dress. He could only hope that Mick would believe him.

Mick would rather not have believed any of it. He had always known, though, that strange things happened at Ninian House. He also knew that Ewan didn't make things up. Neither did Bruce.

Bruce had trotted to the window and was sitting up, with his face turned upward and his eyes alert and attentive. He put his head to one side and lifted one ear, then a paw, and his tail began to swish. When Ewan came back in, Bruce ignored him. He was far more interested in something at the window. Suddenly he rolled over and held up one paw to have his tummy tickled.

"It must be Elspeth," said Ewan. "She must be happier now if she's playing with the dog. And he likes her."

"I thought dogs were scared of ghosties," argued Mick.

"She's not scary, and she's not a ghostie," said Ewan. But Mick, who preferred not to get close to something neither dead nor alive, went to look at the football poster on the closet door instead.

Bruce, sprawled blissfully across the floor, glanced in Mick's direction. He pulled himself together, rolled over, and stood up. He stayed very still, watching Mick, not following him. It was as if he felt the need to stand on guard.

Ewan noticed it. He wished he hadn't. He remembered Elspeth last night, and the last word she had spoken. *"Alex."*

"Breakfast," he said quickly. "I'm starving."

"Then we'll take Bruce up the hill," said Mick. It would be a chance to get out of Ninian House, with its ghosties.

In the kitchen they ate rolls and jam and oatcakes and dropped bits on the floor for Bruce. Ewan's father wandered in, unshaved, and put the kettle on.

"Oh, dear," he said. "Glue." He rubbed uselessly at the sticky marks he had just left on the kettle. Bits of heather, moss, and bracken were sticking to him, too. Ewan and Mick grinned across the table at each other.

"Your mother's gone to the supermarket, I think," he said vaguely to Ewan. "Are you two doing anything today?"

Ewan could tell he was thinking about his lion. He might be wandering about the kitchen, but his mind and heart were in the cellar studio.

"We're taking Bruce out," said Ewan. "We might go to Mick's. And the shop." He glanced at Mick and explained, "I want to find out about the Sutherlands. D'you think they bullied Elspeth?"

"Sutherland?" His father, removing a bit of twig that had somehow fallen into his coffee, suddenly became interested. "There was a Sutherland who lived around here somewhere, a painter. A very good one. Do you mean that Sutherland?"

"Doubt it," said Ewan. His father, sipping his coffee, wandered out again.

"The hill" was a gentle rise behind the house. Bruce ran ahead, busily sniffing from one rabbit hole to the next, finding bits of stick and stone to carry around and drop at their feet. The previous night's storm had left a litter of branches and cones, and muddy patches for Bruce to gallop through. Ewan picked up a snapped branch, overgrown with crumbly gray-green lichen. Bruce lolloped wetly up to him and waited for the throw.

"Sorry, Bruce," said Ewan. "I'm keeping this one." He liked its shape, the delicate lichen, and the clinging cones. "I'll have to keep it away from my dad. If you stand still in our house, you get sculpted." He threw a stone for Bruce and muttered, "At least if that happened, he'd know I was there." He wasn't sure if he wanted Mick to hear that or not.

"You're daft," said Mick. "Your dad's fine. If my dad takes a roll of chicken wire, he makes a run for the hens. Your dad makes a lion. You wouldn't want him fussing over you like a nanny, would you?"

Ewan shrugged, remembering his father's attempts to help him with his homework. He sat on a rock and looked out over Loch Treen. He could imagine sinewy sea monsters rising from it, or even dragons camouflaged in the pine trees behind them. But a lion?

"Why a lion?" he said. "Why does my dad want to make a lion?"

"It's a Scottish heraldic symbol," said Mick.

"I thought that was a thistle." Ewan knew that in the days when knights and nations had their own symbolic pictures—necessary in battle to avoid killing the wrong knight—the usual symbol for Scotland was a thistle.

"It's on the Scottish coat of arms. A Lion Rampant. That means it's standing on its hind legs," Mick said patiently. "Which side of the Borders do you come from? If we're going to Mrs. Craigie's, we'd better move."

Ewan got up and brushed bits of moss from his trousers, which felt uncomfortably damp. They didn't even know if Elspeth's "Alex" was Alex Sutherland, but finding out about him would be a start.

• • •

"Alex Sutherland?" said Mrs. Craigie. She dropped Ewan's change into his hand. "Now what for would you want to know about him? The Sutherlands were a mixed lot. One went into the air force, one into the law, and one into the church, but the one who—" Then the phone rang and more customers came into the shop, and Mick and Ewan gave up, knowing there was no hope of any more help from Mrs. Craigie that day. They were on the way back to Mick's when a car drew up behind them.

"Hi, Mum!" said Ewan. His mother leaned over to open the door.

"I'll drop you at home, Mick," she said. "I'll stop in and see your mum. Put that soggy dog on the floor below the backseats," she added.

At Mick's they all went indoors, where Ewan found Granny Carmichael at the kitchen table, shakily writing a letter. He pulled up a chair beside her.

"That's a bonny wee twig you've got there," she said. She examined the slender branch with fingers almost as dry and frail as the lichen.

"I thought I'd keep it," he said. "I sort of like it. Granny Carmichael, I'm trying to find out about the Sutherlands. There was a boy called Alex, wasn't there?"

"Och, I remember Alex," she said, and chuckled. "The youngest one, and the nicest."

"Really?" said Ewan. It wasn't what he'd expected.

"Aye, and the quietest. He had better manners than

his brothers. I always thought he was a wee bit . . ." She paused and gazed past him into a corner of the room. "A wee bit fey," she said at last.

That didn't help much. Everyone seemed to have their own meaning of "fey."

"What exactly do you mean by 'fey'?"

"Fey? You know. Different. The kind who knows things the rest of us don't. You could call it sixth sense."

He didn't like the next question. But if he had to go on sleeping in that bedroom, he had to know the worst.

"Granny Carmichael, can you tell me what happened to Alex?"

The crumpled face deepened into lines of puzzlement.

"Beg pardon?"

It had been hard enough to ask the first time. He hardly had the nerve to ask again. He spoke slowly, raising his voice for her.

"What happened to Alex Sutherland?"

"Ewan!" called his mother. "Time to go!"

"I don't know what you mean by 'happened,'" said Granny Carmichael. "He's not dead, if that's what you mean. He sends me a Christmas card every year."

Gladness and relief rose up in Ewan and spread into a broad smile across his face. "Great!" he said. "You're the best."

"*Ewan! Now!*"

"I'm coming." He ran out, nearly falling over Bruce. "See you later, Mick."

All he knew about Alex Sutherland was that he was still alive, but that was enough. Whatever he'd done, whatever made Elspeth feel trapped by him, he was not a malicious ghost hovering in Ninian House with evil thoughts. Ewan could have hugged Granny Carmichael, or anyone. He wallowed in the relief as they drove home, while his mother worried aloud about how dark it would be when the winter drew on, and what a long way it was from Mick's house, and whether Ewan was lonely.

At home he ran up the stairs and found his bedroom full of Victorian draperies and ornaments. Then it was his own room again, and he was looking across his bed at his football poster. It was rather good, that poster, but it was past its best.

"What's so fascinating over there?" said Elspeth sharply.

"That poster," said Ewan. "It's getting tatty, and it's last season's, but I like it. I'll put up a new one soon."

"Och, no, I should leave it if I were you."

"Why?" But he didn't wait for an answer. "Elspeth, I've found something out for you. It's about Alex. He's still alive!"

He waited for a cry of joy and relief. She might even thank him for finding it out.

"Oh," she said coldly. "Is he?"

Ewan, who had always wanted brothers and sisters, could now see why family members fell out with each other. If Elspeth had been his sister, they would have fought.

"Is that all you can say?" he said angrily. "I thought you'd be pleased."

"I can't pretend to be," replied Elspeth. "I would if I could."

Ewan sat on the bed and faced the window.

"Come on, then," he said. "If you want me to help, I need to know what's happening. You admitted that you're stuck here because of Alex, but you don't care if he's alive or dead. Tell me about him."

He still couldn't see her, but he could imagine her, curled up and hugging her knees in the window corner. He tried again.

"He was your cousin, wasn't he? I mean, *is* your cousin. He's still alive somewhere else, so how can he make a difference to what happens here?"

"It's not Alex *now,*" she explained. There was a reluctant little sigh, as if she had to tell him but would rather not. "It's something Alex told me then. It was a long time ago. I never asked to know the horrible secret, and I don't suppose you will, either, when you've heard it all. But I'll tell you. Everything."

- 8 -

I came here because my parents didn't want children. When they were wed, Father was already a widower with no family and Mother was near on forty, so they didn't think they'd have any, and they weren't pleased about me. Father was in the civil service, and he was offered a really good posting in India, but they didn't want to take me. I had to stay here with Aunt Stella and Uncle David and the boys. Alan and Adam were already away at school, and Alex . . ."

There was a pause, as if she had to pull herself together.

"When I moved in, this was Alex's room. There wasn't a room for me. I slept in the tiny wee room off the bathroom, but it was far too small."

"It's a cupboard!" exclaimed Ewan.

"There was enough room for a wee bed and the trunk I brought with me, nothing else. I was to move into this bedroom when Alex went away to school, and back into the other one when he came home, and I was looking forward to having this room for my own. I never told anyone, but in my heart I couldn't wait for him to go."

There was a pause, and when she spoke again, her voice was slower and lower-pitched. She must be finding it hard to unfold this old story.

"Mostly, the boys didn't take notice of me. Alan and Adam didn't bother about me one way or another, but that was what I'd expected. They were awful big, almost grown up. But Alex was not so much older than I was. I wanted him to be my friend—I looked forward to that! Like having a big brother, and we'd play together and stand up for each other. Then I found out that he wouldn't speak to me at all. He wasn't cruel—he didn't tease or play tricks or any-thing. He just wanted nothing to do with me. He was awful moody, he spent a lot of time alone in here, and he was always drawing. I don't know if he was any good at it—he didn't often show people his pictures. Certainly not me.

"On the day he had to go away to school, his trunk was downstairs in the hall, all packed and strapped up, with his name on it and his tuck box beside it. Aunt Stella had taken his sheets off the bed and given me the clean ones to bring in. I couldn't wait to have this room to myself.

"It didn't feel like my bedroom yet, but it didn't feel like his, either. All his things were out, or stacked up out of the way. I wondered if there'd be room in the wardrobe for my clothes, so I opened the door and took a wee peep in. Then I got that feeling, the way you do when somebody's watching you.

"I was so scared! I turned sharp round, and there was Alex in the doorway. He had such a look on his face, as if he could burn me to a cinder just by staring at me. I felt myself burning red with shame for sneaking in his room like that. I told him I was just bringing in the sheets, as Aunt Stella had told me to.

"'Did she tell you to look in the wardrobe?' he says, looking like a dog guarding a gate and ready to growl. I was sure he was going to hit me, but he didn't. Then he sat himself down in the basket chair, and he became almost friendly. It was so strange. I couldn't understand it.

"'If this is to be your room now, Elspeth,' he says, 'there are things I need to tell you about it. Especially if you like looking in closets. I should maybe have told you before now, but I know you get scared easily, and I didn't want my wee cousin to be feart. And you needn't be feart, Elspeth, so long as you do exactly as I tell you. This room has secrets, and they must never, ever be told.'

"Of course, I promised not to tell, and he says to me, 'You know how this house shifts about in time? Well, this room does it more than the others. Something must have happened here long ago, something really terrible. A murder, or something even worse. There's a presence in here. But you're not to worry. You're safe, so long as you keep away from the closet.'"

"What, the wall closet?" said Ewan.

"Shh!" said Elspeth, as though it should not even be

mentioned. "Alex said that he used to keep things in there until he realized there was something fearful about it. Whenever he opened it, he felt an evil presence, as if something was lurking in there. Once he heard a noise like something growling."

"That's just the wind in the chimneys," said Ewan uncertainly.

Elspeth's voice became even softer, so that he had to strain to hear her.

"He said he shut the door, but he wasn't fast enough. There was hot breath on his face, and glowing eyes in the dark, and after that he never opened that closet again. And he made me promise never, ever to open it."

"I don't suppose you wanted to," said Ewan.

"I could feel it, after that, every time I came in here," she said. "It was as if that closet was pulling me toward it and taunting me to open it, but I wouldn't. It was better at nights, when I couldn't see it. Then, in October, I got the diphtheria."

"What was that like?"

"I can't remember much about it, except for Aunt Stella bending over me. I couldn't breathe, it was so hard to take a breath, and I could see she was worried, but she couldn't help me. I wanted her to do something, but I couldn't say so. Then I slipped away, and I was so close to the music and the party. . . . Then the time change happened, and I was in the medieval chamber. It only lasted for a moment, but that was *my* moment to go. Letting go is everything. To die you have to let yourself go, like falling and trusting that somebody will catch you."

"Like jumping into a swimming pool," said Ewan.

"But the moment was broken, and I was trapped. And whenever my time has come back, I've tried to let go, but then it's as if something stops me. I can't let go. I can see Alex's face, telling me what's in the closet."

She appeared at last, almost transparent, her face tight and scared. She was shivering.

"It's been shut so long, it's jammed now. Nobody can get it open. But the thing inside, it's just waiting to burst its way out, and one day it will! If I let myself go, will it get me? Or will I release it into the world? And so I . . . can't . . ."

The room began to flicker like an old film.

". . . let go . . ." She quivered. The room quivered, too. Elspeth gathered strength. She choked the words out. ". . . can't let go! I hate Alex! It's his fault! If he'd never told me, I wouldn't have known, and I wouldn't be afraid. I'd be there by now, but I can never do it! I'm trapped forever, and I hate, hate, hate Alex!"

She broke into sobs so loud that Ewan thought she would be heard all over the house. He ran to the window, but she vanished as his father ran into the room without knocking.

"Is this room going wild as well? This house! How can I work when the studio keeps changing and the lights go on and off all day!"

"Dad!" yelled Ewan. "Don't you think of anything but your sculptures?"

They glared at each other like boxers from their corners. They both knew that they had overstepped the permitted lines, Ewan's father by bursting into the room and Ewan by shouting at him.

"Sorry," muttered Ewan reluctantly. "You might have knocked." His father's face softened a bit.

"I think we should do something about lunch, don't you?" he said carefully. "Your mum brought some fresh bread and smoked cheese with her. Sound good?"

The first step had been taken. Ewan accepted it.

"I'll be down in a minute," he said, and as his father left, he turned back to the window. Elspeth had disappeared, but he knelt down beside the corner where she had been.

"Elspeth," he said, "I have to go now. But I'll soon be back. I think I can see a way through this. We'll get you out." He took the lichen-covered branch he had found in the morning and left it there, where he had last seen her.

Lunch was a soup-and-sandwich affair. Mum came to the table yawning and ordered Dad to change out of his scruffy old sweater, otherwise he'd drop bits of lichen in his soup.

"But it's beautiful lichen," he said, pulling the sweater over his head.

"I brought some home," said Ewan. "But it's in my room and it's to keep, so don't touch it."

"Mick's mum showed me their holiday cottage," said Mum. She stirred her soup, and Ewan knew she was seeing it as a design for wallpaper. "Lucky for you to have the snooker table in there."

"Snooker table?" Dad looked up with sudden interest. Ewan wondered if he really did want to play snooker or if he was thinking about buying some table legs for his lion. "Do you think I could go and play snooker there?"

Ewan hesitated. Snooker was to do with Mick and himself, not parents, but he knew he was supposed to say yes. Maybe this was one of the "Try to be a good father" days, but it was nice that he wanted to try.

"Maybe," he said. "I'll check with Mick."

When lunch was over, he phoned Mick and found him all too happy to have another player at the snooker table. Then he ran upstairs.

"Elspeth," he called, "this is important!"

He couldn't see her and she didn't speak, but the lichen branch was pushed across the floor toward him. He picked it up and carried it to the window, and Elspeth appeared, holding out her hand for it.

"I've worked it all out," he said. "There's nothing to be afraid of." She looked at him as if he were the village idiot and hadn't understood a word she'd said, but he went on.

"Alex told you there was something terrible in that closet," he said. "Do you know what that sounds like to me? It sounds like the bogeyman. He was saying, 'Don't open that door, or a monster will get you!' Can't you see,

Elspeth? I think Alex had something hidden in there. His supply of sweets, maybe, or some sports stuff, something that he didn't want anyone to find, so he told you never to open the door or something horrible would get you. You believed him. You still do. You've been unable to let go for all these years in case something gets you, but it can't. There's nothing there."

She stared into his eyes. Her face was set and hard, and her voice flat as ice on a loch.

"It's real. I can feel it," she said. "And you can feel it, too." She vanished.

Ewan put the branch on his desk. "Suit yourself." He shrugged. "I'm going to Mick's. I have to take my father for a game of snooker." And he looked hard at the closet before he left, just to show that he wasn't afraid of it. But as he turned his back on it he could feel it, as if it was watching him.

Mick's family welcomed Simon Dart as readily as they welcomed everyone, but Ewan felt embarrassed at having him there. He quickly hustled him out of the way to the cottage, where Mick watched their game of snooker. Dad proved surprisingly good at it, and Ewan, who had wondered whether to let his father win, soon found himself struggling. Ewan did win at last, but only because his father missed an easy shot.

"I'll leave you two to have a game," his father said. "See you later, Ewan."

Left alone, Mick and Ewan set up the table again while Ewan told Mick Elspeth's story.

"I think it was just one of those bogeyman tales," he said, "but she doesn't believe me. All the same, it was a nasty thing to do, scaring her like that."

"I reckon he couldn't see how much it would upset her," said Mick. "Anyway, if anyone had spun me that story, I'd have been straight into that closet like a ferret up a spout."

"Yes, so would I, but Elspeth isn't like that. She's scared of her own shadow."

"Have you tried opening the closet?"

"First thing I did when we moved in. It's jammed solid. Dad can't shift it, either."

"Is it locked?"

"It's got a keyhole, but it's so tight you can't see if it's been locked. It might as well be. If it wasn't stuck fast, I could just open it and show her there's nothing in there." He stood back from the table. "You have first shot."

"Take a chisel to it," said Mick, lining up his shot.

"That might work," admitted Ewan, though the idea made him uneasy. "I just wish she'd believe me."

"She might believe her cousin Alex," said Mick. The colored triangle of balls scattered.

"Alex?" asked Ewan.

"Why not?" Pleased with his shot, Mick straightened up. "He's still alive. Granny gets a Christmas card from him every year, so I expect she sends him one, too. Ask her where he is. If we can get Alex to come back here and tell her it was only a scare story, and say he's sorry, she'll be all right."

It seemed a good idea—until Ewan imagined himself putting it into practice. "So I phone a total stranger and tell him I've found a ghost in his old house and will he come and talk to it, please?"

"Why not? Granny told you he was a wee bit fey, and he's lived in your weirdo house before. He might understand."

Ewan leaned against the wall and inspected his snooker cue. "He wasn't very understanding with Elspeth, was he?"

"That was when he was young." Mick folded his arms. "It's obvious you never had wee sisters, nor wee cousins, either, peeking into closets and pushing their noses in.

"It's your turn. Are you going to take this shot or aren't you?"

– 9 –

It was growing dark when Ewan picked up his jacket to go home. He looked at the address written on the back of an envelope in Granny Carmichael's small, shivery handwriting.

"*Rev A Sutherland, 3 The Wynd, Inver, Argyll,*" he read. "He would have to be a vicar, or a minister, or a chief churchy, or something."

"What's wrong with that?" said Mick.

"I don't know, but he's sure to be awkward," said Ewan, who didn't have much experience of churches. "But he's Alex, so I'll have to get in touch. Pity she doesn't have the phone number."

"He'll be retired by now," said Mick. "Maybe he's stopped being awkward."

Not only a vicar, but an old vicar, thought Ewan as he rode his bike home. Of course Alex was old. Elspeth would be over seventy if she'd lived, though he couldn't picture her as an elderly woman and didn't want to. As he put his bike away, he saw that the lights were on in the kitchen.

"I'm doing a really special meal," called his father.

Ewan glanced uncertainly at his mother. "Why? Have you won another contract or something, or has Dad got a commission?"

She shrugged. "Goodness knows. It's nothing to do with me. He just decided he wanted to do something special for supper. We're even eating in the dining room, cloth on the table and everything. Did you ever say you liked Chinese food?"

"Yes." He nodded enthusiastically. "Love it." He didn't add that when he'd said that, he was thinking of the take-out restaurant near their last home. There was a clatter and a gasp of "Ouch!" from the kitchen.

"Do you think he wants help?" asked Ewan.

"I'll go. You stay out of the way. Set the table if you like."

The meal was very good. Dad looked flustered as he brought it to the table, and was covered with bits of noodle instead of moss, but he smiled valiantly as he carried in the dishes. There was a lot of food, and it didn't taste the same as the meals from the take-out place, but they all enjoyed it. They hardly had room for the apple crumble and ice cream that followed, but his dad said they ought to have dessert. When they were done, Ewan stacked the dishes and took them to the kitchen.

The kitchen was, to his surprise, immaculately clean and tidy. Then he realized he was in a time change and the bare floor, scrubbed table, and heavy crockery belonged to Elspeth's time, not his own. He waited for it to slip back to the present.

It did, and he wished it hadn't. A mound of pans, bowls, and spatulas in the sink appeared to be climbing out. Every item in the kitchen must have been used, and the wok had singed a hole in the counter. Opened packets tipped and spilled across the table; vegetable peelings were tumbled in a heap. Ewan wanted to say they were wonderful natural materials, but decided he'd better not. His mother came in behind him.

"I think we should *all* clean up together," she said.

"It'll take all three of us," said Ewan.

It took a long time, but it was fun, all of them together in the kitchen making silly jokes about noodles and teasing Dad about the bits of mushroom stuck to the inside of the microwave. Finally, Ewan went upstairs and flopped on his bed.

"Hi, Elspeth," he said. He wasn't going to tell her about the search for Alex Sutherland, not yet. It would only worry her.

"You've been out for ages," she said. "This morning I thought you'd be shut in here all day, after the way you spoke to your father. Did you get a skelping?"

"No!" He laughed. "He doesn't hit me. He's been all right. In fact, he's been a bit strange."

"If I'd spoken to my father like that, or my uncle, or any of them, I'd have been lathered."

"It's different now," said Ewan, who disliked the idea of anyone hitting her. "Parents don't do that so much—at least, most of them don't."

"I think your father's lovely. I wish he was my father. And your mum, she's lovely, too."

"Hang on." Ewan sat up. "How do you know anything about them? You're always in here."

"Yes, and I'm here when you're not, Mr. Know-all," she returned. "I'm here when your dad comes in and puts your clean washing on your bed—did you think the fairies brought it? Who do you think sweeps the carpet with that noisy machine? I can tell your parents care about you just from the way they handle your clothes and smooth the quilt and shake up your pillow. And I'm here at night, when they peek in on you."

"I didn't know they peeked—I mean, looked—in on me."

"They always come in here before they go to bed," said Elspeth, with the satisfaction of knowing something he didn't. "You wouldn't know, because it's when you're asleep. Your father takes a long look at you, and he usually says something like 'We're so lucky,' and he means that they're lucky to have you. And she comes in after him, and sometimes they whisper a bit, and talk about what you've done at school, and whether they think you like it here. Your mum says she'd like to be with you more, but she needs to work, and your dad's always going on about whether he should be around for you, or if you'd rather be left alone. He doesn't want to make too much fuss over you."

"You're not making this up, are you?" said Ewan, but he knew she wasn't.

"Cross my heart," she said. "Aye, and they say you talk to yourself. They're a wee bit worried about that."

"They must have heard me talking to you."

"Aye, but they don't know about me, so they think you're talking to yourself because you're too much alone. Nobody was fashed about me. Mostly, it was the servants looked after me. Some of them were good to me, but they were awful busy."

"Your aunt stayed with you when you were dying," said Ewan.

"Aye, she was good to me then. She was never cruel nor mean, nor anything of that sort. She'd just rather I wasn't there. I'd have given anything, Ewan, to be like you, with your parents!"

It made sense. Now he came to think of it, he'd rather have his own parents than anybody else's, even Mick's.

"Did you have any friends?"

"Sometimes I played with the children where your friend lives. And I had an imaginary friend."

Ewan, who had done the same thing when he was younger, smiled. "What did you call him—or her?"

"Ninian. After the saint and the house. He was very big and strong, and he was always there to defend me, but he was fun, too, and I could play with him."

"Sounds like a big dog."

"Och, no! He was a lion. Ninian, my lion. But I do like dogs. Do you think your friend might bring his dog here again?"

"Maybe." What was it about Ninian House that made Elspeth and his father dream of lions? He swung his legs over the side of the bed. "I'm just going to make a phone call."

The operator gave him the number, and he tapped it out as he wondered what to say. How could he talk to a total stranger about an almost ghost? When a cultured Scots voice gave a recorded message, he was almost relieved.

"I'm sorry, but neither Alex nor Flora Sutherland is available to take your call," said a woman's voice. "Please leave your name, number, and message after the tone."

He thought quickly as the machine beeped and whirred. He gave his name and number and added, "It's very important. I live at Loch Treen, in Ninian House. I need to speak to Alex Sutherland."

When Ewan went to bed that night, his room was totally dark. That was one of the problems of walking into the Middle Ages. He had expected a warm bedroom with a lamp glowing, his bed waiting, and soft carpet under his feet. Instead, he found blackness and a freezing floor. There was a *creak, creak* from the corner, which sounded like the rocking of a cradle. He *hoped* it was only the rocking of a cradle. He heard his mother downstairs.

"I wish it wouldn't do that," she snapped. But as soon as she'd said it, Ewan was in his own room again. After the bare chamber, it seemed luxuriously comfortable. He scrambled into bed, then remembered something he'd meant to ask Elspeth.

"Elspeth, why is it that, when the house does a slip, everything goes completely back to normal? Nothing's changed. The electricity doesn't go off. The computer doesn't crash, the clocks don't need resetting. Why not?"

"Because the power isn't affected," she said simply. "It's still there. Your time is still there. You just can't see what it does anymore."

The lichen twig, which had been lying on the floor, stood on end, stayed for a second or two, and fell over.

"It looks spooky when you do that," said Ewan. "It looks as if it does it by itself."

There was a giggle, and the twig flew across the room. Ewan caught it in one hand. Elspeth was becoming a bit like a kid sister. Something new occurred to him.

"Elspeth, since you died—or not died—have you asked anybody else to help you? Anybody before me?"

"I tried," came Elspeth's voice. "I tried hard, but none of them could see me or hear me. You're the first."

"I wonder why." Ewan felt singled out and privileged.

"Doesn't mean you're magic or special or anything," she said primly. "Maybe we're just a bit the same."

"Don't talk rubbish!"

"It's true. I belong half in one world and half in the other. Work it out for yourself, you lazy Englishman."

"I'm a Borderer," he replied.

"Aye," said Elspeth. "Exactly. Good night to you."

She had said all she was going to say. Ewan turned over and reached for a book. He read for a long time before turning out the light.

Normally at this point he would sink into a fantasy in which he scored a winning goal or saved someone from drowning. Tonight was different.

Usually he lay on his right side with his back to the closet. Tonight he could feel it behind him, out of his sight. Behind the poster was a door. Behind the door was either a black and gaping space or nameless terror. It ate into his back.

He rolled over and looked at the ceiling. It was Elspeth who feared the closet, not him. The whole point of getting Alex here was to convince her that there was absolutely nothing to be afraid of. All the same, it kept him awake. He remembered Bruce that morning, standing guard.

"It's only a closet," he told himself. He'd slept in this room for months without harm. He turned the light back on and picked up his book again, lying on his left side this time. If there was anything sinister in there, he'd rather face it than have it creeping from behind.

In the morning it all seemed ridiculous, and not worth mentioning to Mick or Elspeth. There was no reply from

Alex Sutherland, and that worried him. In the afternoon Mick came over, and Bruce, carrying a ball in his mouth, rolled over on his back by the window and wagged his tail at somebody they couldn't see. The ball fell from his mouth and rolled across the floor. Bruce chased after it and dropped it, sometimes at Mick's feet, sometimes at Ewan's, and sometimes at the window. Then Mick rolled it toward the closet. Bruce ran after it, changed his mind, and sat down with his head to one side.

"What's the matter with you?" said Mick.

"He shouldn't be cooped up in here," said Ewan hastily. "He should be outside on the hill. Let's all get outside."

They took Bruce for a long walk, and Ewan picked up branches and pebbles that he thought might be useful to his father. He was beginning to like finding lichens, with their crisp, gray-green coral delicacy. They sat on a tree trunk while the evening gold and apricot spread into the sky and shone in the loch.

"I have to get home now, with Bruce, before it gets dark," said Mick. "See you tomorrow."

Ewan carried his armful of rough branches home. He arrived as his father emerged from the cellar studio with his arms full of dried reeds and rushes. His mother sat on the stairs with her chin in her hands and said that one of them was as bad as the other, and why didn't they just bring the whole hill indoors, and the loch, too, and they could all move into the garden. But they had a good time sitting on the floor together and turning over the branches, examining the crinkled stars of lichen, the delicate cones and clusters of needles.

"What are you going to do with them?" asked his mother.

"They're for Dad's lion," Ewan said, and his father's face took on a smile that was touched and pleased. He looked as if he wasn't sure whether to put his arm around Ewan or not. Perhaps, thought Ewan, this place is as normal as it needs to be. And that goes for us, too.

Later, when he was finishing his homework and his books were spread all over the floor, his father came upstairs. Ewan hoped he wouldn't try to help.

"Want any help, Ewan?" he offered.

"I've finished it all, Dad. You go back to your lion."

Dad nodded, went to the door, and turned back.

"Your mum and I worry a bit, you know. You're alone up here a lot."

"I've been out all afternoon with Mick," Ewan reminded him.

"Yes, but . . . I sometimes wonder if . . . you need to be with more people your own age. And perhaps you should live in a normal house."

"I like this house. I'd like it more if it wasn't the only one here, but I like it."

His father hesitated, as if he felt there was more to be said. "Have you got enough space for all your books in here?" he said at last.

"Yes, Dad. It's fine." But his father still hovered.

"Pity about that closet."

Ewan jerked around in his chair. His father's gaze was fixed on the closet.

"It won't open," said Ewan quickly. He turned hot, then cold.

"It never did," said his father. "Let's have another go."

"Just leave it, you might tear my poster, it's my best one," Ewan said desperately, because it was all he could think of. He could feel his heart beating harder.

"I won't tear your poster." His father took hold of the doorknob and pulled.

Ewan curled his fingers so tightly that his nails hurt him. He could not look away from his father, but from the corner of his eye he saw Elspeth, curled up on the floor, shivering, her hands over her head. The room flashed into her time, then back again.

The door still didn't open. Dad jerked it and heaved against it. A thin cold line of sweat tickled the back of Ewan's neck.

His father took a chisel from his pocket. Typical of a sculptor, thought Ewan. He always carried a chisel.

"Don't, Dad, please don't. You'll damage the wood." But his father had already slipped the chisel against the door.

Ewan didn't often go to church, but he had seen people make the sign of the cross. He did it now, though he wasn't sure why, and tried to think of a prayer.

The door stayed solid. His father, red in the face, gave up. Ewan forced a smile.

"Stick with your lion, Dad," he said.

As soon as his father had gone, he wondered what he'd been so worried about. He knew there was nothing harmful in the closet, so why was he scared? And, come to think of it, why hadn't Alex Sutherland phoned?

Perhaps there was something wrong with the answering machine. Maybe his message had been erased by mistake. Maybe something had happened to stop him from reaching Alex, just as the storm had nearly kept him from Elspeth on the night of the power cut. Before he went to bed, he wrote a letter to Alex Sutherland to post on the way to school. By now, he knew he didn't just need help for Elspeth. It was for himself, too.

- 10 -

Autumn took Loch Treen by storm. Merciless winds and rain rushed in from the north, tearing at the trees and whipping up the loch. Going out in the mornings, Ewan and Mick were swept haphazardly along the track. Coming home, they huddled their shoulders and staggered against the wind with their heads down and their hands in their pockets. Sharp rain spat and stung their faces. Every day after school, Ewan stayed at Mick's house until his mother arrived.

"We must have been crazy to move here," she would mutter as she struggled to the car. "Are you sure you're happy here, Ewan? *Sure?*"

There was always a log fire at Ninian House. Drafts would rush down the chimneys, sending gusts of smoke and sparks into the hearth. Ewan's father worked intensely to complete his lion, though he always stopped to make a hot drink when Ewan and his mother came home. At night, gales tore twigs from the trees and tossed them against the windows. Gusts of wind roared in the chimneys or whimpered like the crying of a sad child.

The house changed its time more often than ever. Warlords gathered in the hall. Sheep and cattle appeared in the kitchen. Ewan's room was sometimes the bare medieval room with the cradle, sometimes Victorian, and, more often, Elspeth's room. The whole house favored the 1930s. "They still had marble washstands!" cried his mother in delight.

"I really like this house," Ewan said to Elspeth one November evening as the bedroom became hers. "It's confusing and frustrating and too far away from anywhere, but I'd hate to have to leave it. It's trying to help you. It's trying to get back to your moment."

"Sometimes I think I'll never be free," she said. "I'm stuck here forever."

"We'll get you out. Promise."

"We?"

Ewan, leafing through his homework books, looked up in the direction of her voice. It wasn't fair that she could see him when he couldn't see her.

"You said 'we,'" repeated Elspeth. "Who's 'we'?"

"Me and Mick," he said. He still hadn't heard from Alex Sutherland.

"Mick's all right, but you get some strange people," she said. "When the Sutherlands were still here, after I died, they invited someone to stay for the weekend. She had a crystal, and she wore a long scarf around her neck, and it turned out she was some sort of a . . . what's the word . . ."

"Nutcase?" offered Ewan.

"Medium," she said firmly. "A medium. She said there was an unquiet spirit in the house. She couldn't do a thing about me. She made me dizzy and seasick, but she didn't do me any good. There've been others since, the same sort of thing, but they couldn't get me through. Nobody can."

"Somebody will," said Ewan.

"Nobody who's likely to come here. And I've had enough of—what are they called again?"

"You just told me. Mediums."

"No, the thing you said before—nutcases—to last me forever. Forever," she repeated softly. "Forever."

He saw her. She was at the window, pressing both hands against the glass, her back to him, her face so close that if she could breathe, she would have misted it. He couldn't see her face, but he knew how she would look, yearning and hurting. In a place like this, it should be easy to slip from one world to the next. It was only the closet, or something in it, or about it, that held her back, as if that yawning black space could be bigger than the whole room. He had told Elspeth that there was nothing there to be afraid of. He had told himself, too, but he couldn't quite believe it.

Come on, Alex, he thought. You haven't phoned, you haven't written. Where are you?

"Alex didn't like this room after that," she said suddenly, and Ewan was caught off guard.

"What made you think of Alex?"

"I don't know. Something just put him in my head. He didn't like it after I died here, and when Alan went to the university he moved into the big room with Adam. Perhaps he's thinking about me." And she vanished, like a wisp of smoke.

"She said Alex must be thinking of her," Ewan said to Mick as they battled their way from the school bus the next day. The north wind had a dry taste of ice in it. "Maybe that means he's got my message, and he's going to do something about it."

"It's been a week," said Mick. "Tomorrow's Saturday. Maybe he's on holiday."

"Nobody goes on holiday in November."

"Loads of retired folk do. It's cheaper then. They go abroad for the fine weather. Some of them are away for months."

"Thanks, Mick." Ewan kicked a pebble and squinted into the wind toward Ninian House. "She'll be here all winter if that's happened."

"Is she being a pain?"

"No, she's all right. I've got used to her." He knew the truth of this as he said it. "But she's not happy—that's why she has to go. I talk to her a lot. She reckons my parents think I'm talking to myself and going around the twist. If I haven't heard from Alex by tomorrow, I'll phone again."

Scowling against a sudden burst of sleet, they said little

more until they reached Mick's house. They'd hardly taken their wet shoes and socks off before Ewan's mother arrived. She struggled into the house carrying two enormous cans of paint ("they're just leftovers from the Livingstone Gallery, but you might be able to use them for the cottage") and left with Ewan, a bag of onions, and two jars of home-made chutney. She seemed to be getting on really well with Mick's mother.

Ninian House looked strangely different when they reached home. The light behind the windows was paler, and it was alive. It moved and danced, like curtains in a breeze. They tiptoed to the window and looked in.

They saw the leaping of the log fire, rugs on the floor, and a high-backed chair. An old woman sat with a small boy in her lap. There was a dog, too—a wolfhound, gray and rangy, with his head resting on the old woman's knee and his eyes on her face, but the small boy gazed intently into the fire. Then they vanished, and it was only the sitting room again.

"They never last long," said Ewan sadly.

"They're not meant to. Come and get warm." She ushered him inside. "I wonder which story she was telling him."

"Bonnie Prince Charlie and Flora. Robert the Bruce and the spider. Or *Tam Lin*."

"*Tam Lin*'s different. That's a folktale," she said. Only it seemed to Ewan that the stories were all the same, but he couldn't have explained how.

Saturday brought no word from Alex Sutherland. After supper, he tried phoning again.

"Hello?" said a young woman's voice. Ewan, expecting the recorded message, was caught off guard. He gabbled and stammered before he managed to say what he wanted.

"I'm afraid they're both away just now," said the voice at the other end. "I'm Joy, their daughter. Are you the laddie who left a message on the machine?"

"Yes. I wrote a letter, too."

"I'm sorry, son, but they've been away visiting some of the family in England. Then they're coming home tomorrow night and flying out to America in the morning, for two months. My dad's got an exhibition of his paintings there."

Ewan thought of Elspeth, trapped in Ninian House. He felt useless and worn out.

"Tell you what could help, though," she went on brightly. "They're staying in Dumfries tonight, and Dad's taking the morning service in Kilally tomorrow morning. That's near Loch Treen is it not? If you want to catch him, you could go to the church there. It's . . . just let me check . . . it's a ten o'clock service."

"That's great!" said Ewan. The hope that had left him rushed in with new energy. "I'll be there. Thanks very much."

"By the way," she said, "is everything all right at Ninian House?"

"It's the same as always, thanks," he said. "'Bye, for now."

The same as always. In 1937 Alex Sutherland had left Ninian House and a lonely, frightened little girl. She was still there. If he couldn't help, she could be there forever.

It would be a long bike ride and an early start to get to Kilally, but Ewan worked out that he wouldn't have to be there for the beginning of the church service, which he didn't want to go to anyway. If Kilally was anything like Loch Treen, the ten o'clockers would be coming out of church at about eleven, and they'd all stand about outside and chat with the minister. He'd leave early, though, just in case. Perhaps he should prepare the ground with Elspeth just a little.

"Elspeth," he said when he was upstairs, "just suppose that I could find someone who could help you to escape, someone really safe. Would you mind if I told him about you?"

"I've told you I don't like cases of nuts," she said cautiously.

"No, I mean somebody who really understood. What if he was a priest? You said once that a priest would be all right."

"A nice priest, who really understood what he was doing?" she said wistfully. "He could help."

"He could help just by proving to you that there's nothing to be afraid of in that closet," said Ewan.

"Why won't Bruce go near it, then?" she demanded. "Why do you always go to bed facing it? You can feel it behind you. I was the same when I slept in this room."

"Well, maybe that's why," he said, trying and failing to be patient. "Maybe it's because you make such a fuss about it, you've got me as daft as you are yourself." He made himself busy sorting out the socks that were the most comfortable ones for long bike rides and tossed them onto the bed, ready for tomorrow. "Whatever's in there, it can't be scarier than my socks. Come on, Elspeth, lighten up. Laugh for a change!"

She didn't. It occurred to Ewan that he'd heard her giggle, but he'd never heard her laugh, not really laugh. Maybe that was part of the trouble.

"You're going *where?*" asked his mother as Ewan finished breakfast next morning. "It'll take you hours! Can't it wait? I have to take some bedspreads to Blackwater Hall this morning, but I can take you this afternoon."

"This afternoon's too late. I'll be back for lunch. It's not that far."

"Take a drink. Take something to eat. Take a jacket, in case it rains." And she called after him when he was almost out of earshot, "Take *care!*"

In Ninian House, Elspeth hovered at her window. Ewan's mother put on her jacket to drive to Blackwater Hall. In the basement, Simon patiently crushed and glued and wove leaves into the almost completed lion. The wind whistled teasingly down the chimneys. The hall suddenly filled with warriors, who vanished again like a dream.

. . .

Ewan pedaled steadily along the winding roads. The wind was behind him, so it was an easy run, and he was enjoying the speed and smoothness of the autumn day. He tried to imagine what he would say to Alex Sutherland, who hadn't even received his messages.

"Hello, my name's Ewan. I live at Ninian House. Remember your cousin Elspeth? Well, she's still there."

"Hello, Reverend Sutherland, are you any good with ghosts? Because there's this ghost in my house, but she isn't really a ghost, that's the trouble, and she needs to escape, and you have to help her because it's your fault she's there."

He was making good time and was thinking of stopping for a drink. Then he saw the red triangle in the road and the set of lights ahead.

At Ninian House, the bedroom fell back to the Middle Ages. Ewan's father straightened his aching back and decided it was time to take a break. He locked the door and began to walk up the hill.

Ewan looked at his watch. If he'd known there would be construction work here, he would have ridden faster. There was nothing to do now but wait with one foot on the ground and watch the traffic from the other direction roll slowly past. He'd have to race to make up the time. When the light changed, he was ready for a fast start and accelerated. There was a challenge in swiftness, and he loved the effort and the joy of speed, while at the back of his mind the script still rehearsed itself—"Reverend Sutherland, may I have a word with you in private? My name's Ewan Dart, I live at Ninian House . . ."

He didn't see the lamb until he was already around the corner. He tightened the brakes, put down his foot, and fell.

The helmet saved him, but the first rush of pain knocked the breath out of him. He squeezed his eyes shut against it. The sound of the lamb bleating as it scurried off seemed far away.

Count backward from a high number, he thought. Three hundred, two hundred and ninety-nine, two hundred and ninety-eight—by the time he reached two hundred and eighty, he could breathe almost normally, and the pain was bearable. He sat up, gasped at the stab in his shoulder, and cautiously moved his arm. He could still bend his elbow and flex his fingers. The stinging in his leg came from a deep graze, which, as he inspected it, was already turning blue and purple. The tracksuit trousers and socks had protected his ankle from a worse bruising, but the one they had was bad enough.

He limped to the bike, straightened it, and climbed on. It was a wobbly start. Every move hurt his left shoulder, but the determination not to fall again made him tighten his mouth and persist. Every pressure of his foot on the pedal renewed the pain in his leg and ankle. Even leaning into the handlebars tormented his shoulder. But he could see the church tower of Kilally. He went on counting backward—two hundred and fifty-nine, two hundred and fifty-eight—and wondered if the cars passing him in the other direction were churchgoers on their way home.

At Loch Treen, Lizzie drove past the post office and along the single-track road to Blackwater Hall. Simon took in the view west of the hill and could not resist exploring a little farther. At Ninian House, somebody rang the doorbell and waited for an answer.

Two hundred and thirty-five. Nearly there. Ewan slowed down outside the whitewashed church with its neat garden and the low stone wall around it. To his relief, the church door still stood open, and a few people hung about gossiping outside. All right now, he thought. It will be all right. He put his foot on the ground and dismounted, swinging his weight from the bike.

A roar of pain rushed through his left arm and made his head spin so that he stumbled to the wall. There, sitting with his head down, he fought the tearing pain in his shoulder and the throbbing in his leg.

At Ninian House, the door was not answered. The figure on the doorstep turned and walked away.

• • •

Someone was talking to Ewan. When he could think further than the pain, he looked up, and there were kind faces around him. They were asking questions, but the words at the front of his mind were the only ones he could say.

"I need Alex Sutherland."

"Och, it's Ewan! Ewan from Ninian House! What are you doing here? What have you done to yourself?"

It was Mrs. Craigie. She fussed over him, narrowing her eyes in concern as she looked at the blood on his sock and asked him why he was holding his shoulder.

"It hurts a bit—I fell off my bike. Where's Alex Sutherland?"

She was very gently helping him off with his jacket, but he wouldn't let her touch his shoulder. His arm was stiffening all the time.

"Cold towels," said somebody in the crowd. "Or ice."

"Alex!" insisted Ewan. "I have to see him!"

"Reverend Sutherland?" asked Mrs. Craigie. "He's long away. He hardly stopped after the service. That's right, Ewan, you put your head down if you feel dizzy."

But Ewan put his head down because he could not hold it up any longer.

In the drafty emptiness of Ninian House, Elspeth stood invisible at the window with the lichen twig in her hand. The closet creaked behind her.

- 11 -

It's a good thing I was here," remarked Mrs. Craigie. They managed somehow to get the bike into the back of her car, and Ewan limped into the passenger seat, strapping himself in carefully to protect the shoulder that was too painful to bear the seat belt. Mrs. Craigie had insisted on applying first aid to the graze, and to a bad cut on his wrist that Ewan hadn't even noticed. "You could never have cycled home, not in that state."

She glanced in the mirror and drove off. "I came all this way to hear Alex Sutherland preach," she said. "I didn't think you were a churchgoer."

"I'm not. I had to meet him. There was something I needed to . . . to discuss."

"Is that so? Well, I daresay whatever it was, it'll bide a little longer."

Bide a little longer. Elspeth had been "biding" long enough.

"That's where I came off my bike," he remarked as they

drove by the spot. The lamb didn't even look up. "And there's construction farther on."

"Aye, they're doing the roads on a Sunday," she said with a frown. "I can't see why, with six perfectly good working days, they have to do that on the Lord's Day. They never used to."

But they did today, thought Ewan, so I had to hurry, and the lamb just had to be there today when I came round that bend too fast. The first time he had raced to help Elspeth, he had been caught in torrential rain and darkness. It was as if . . .

Bruce wouldn't go near the closet. Elspeth believed there was something terrible in the closet. Something terrible *out* of the closet would be even worse. Something that would go to any lengths to stop him. And now there would be no Alex Sutherland to put everything right—if even Alex Sutherland could. Ewan shuddered.

"I'll take you to your door," said Mrs. Craigie as they drove past the Loch Treen post office, "but are you by chance up to popping in at the McPhersons' on the way? I ought to see how Granny Carmichael is. You can stay in the car if you'd rather."

"I'm feeling better now—I'll come in with you," he said. Having failed to find Alex, he didn't really want to see anyone, even Mick, just yet, but it didn't seem right to sit outside in the car. A sense of relief soothed him as they took the road along the side of the loch. Soft mist welcomed them. The loch was lapping gently. There was

Ninian House in the distance on its rock at the far end, and Mick's whitewashed cottage with smoke rising from the chimney. Mrs. Craigie parked outside the holiday cottage.

"That's your parents' car, isn't it?" she said. "And I don't know who the other car belongs to. We'd better not stop long if they have company." But Mick had already seen them and was running outside with Bruce beside him. Ewan eased himself painfully from the car.

"Ewan, get yourself in, quick! What do you mean, you can't? Well, quick as you can, then!" Ewan hobbled stiffly to the house, trying to keep up with Mick, who was suddenly finding everything exciting and not taking the slightest notice of Ewan's injuries.

He felt it before he saw anything—there was an atmosphere crackling with happy excitement, like a party. Granny Carmichael, with a broad smile on her face, was listening to the fast, eager conversation between Ewan's father and a man with neat white hair, a little beard, and remarkably deep brown eyes. He wore a dark suit and a gray shirt with a clerical collar.

"Why, Alex!" said Mrs. Craigie. "So this is where you were rushing off to after the kirk!"

"Ewan," said his father, and his voice was warm with delight, "this is Reverend Alex Sutherland. *The* Alex Sutherland. The painter."

With a bit of help from Mick, Ewan lowered himself into the nearest chair.

"I've been all the way to Kilally trying to find you," he said.

"And you had a fight with the road in the process, by the look of you," said Alex Sutherland. He had a crisp accent and a warmhearted manner, and Ewan liked him at once. It seemed that everyone had relaxed and was sharing infectious happiness because Alex was there. Ewan tried to imagine him as the quiet cousin who had brought crippling fear to Elspeth, but it was impossible.

"I called at Ninian House earlier," Alex went on, "but there was nobody in. I was hoping to see it again, and maybe take a look in my old bedroom."

"You can come now if you like," said Ewan eagerly. "I'll take you there." His mother began to say something, but he interrupted. "I've got my key—I'll let us in."

"Let's get you loaded into my car, then," said Alex.

Mick waved them off, and they drove back to Ninian House. When they were on their way, Alex began.

"Now, Ewan. I woke up this morning with the picture of Ninian House in my head and its name on my lips, and I knew I had to be there, fast. I haven't felt easy since then. And now I find that you got on your bike and cycled all the way to Kilally to get to the church, and I presume you didn't do that just for the joy of hearing my sermon. You were so determined to find me, you went whizzing off like a collie at a cat show and got yourself injured, and then kept going. Whatever you want to ask me about, it must be important."

They reached Ninian House, and he parked the car. "Am I right?"

"You're right."

"Bull's-eye!" He opened the door. "So do please tell me what's going on. Take as long as you like."

So, as they went into the house, Ewan told Alex everything about Elspeth. When he had finished, there was a long silence. Alex sat with his hands folded and his eyes closed, and Ewan didn't dare speak to him.

"Poor, poor Elspeth," he said at last. "Little Elspeth. I would never have hurt her, not deliberately. If only . . . I had no idea. I'd forgotten all about that closet. All about it. Poor little Elspeth. How terrible for her."

He closed his eyes. Then he opened them, gave himself a shake, and said, "Ewan, do you know what a peterman is?"

"Peterman?" Ewan thought hard, trying to remember where he'd heard that word before. "Elspeth said something about a peterman once, but I never found out what it was."

"It's a safecracker, a lock-picker, that sort of thing," said Alex. "In old crime stories, the peterman was the one with the skeleton keys, to open doors for the rest of the gang. The tradition is that St. Peter has the keys of heaven. That's why keys are a sign of St. Peter. In old stained-glass windows, you see him holding a bunch of keys as if he's waiting for everyone to go home so he can lock up. So criminals came to use that word, 'peterman,' for somebody who opens doors. Poor old St. Peter! Lovely friend of God, and they name criminals after him!"

Ewan nodded and wondered what all this had to do with Elspeth.

"Now, I don't go around picking locks and breaking into safes," Alex went on, "but, in another way, I'm a bit of a peterman. I open doors. When someone like Elspeth is stuck between one stage and the next, I'm sometimes able to help them through—or open a door, as you might say."

"So you're used to talking to ghosts?" said Ewan hopefully.

"Yes. I do a lot of talking to ghosts."

"Can you help Elspeth?"

"I'll certainly try. I suspect you've probably done most of it already."

"I haven't done anything. Elspeth told me not to do anything but be there."

"Exactly. Good, sensible girl. Excuse me a minute."

He left the room, knelt beside the chest in the hall, and prayed. It was only then that Ewan realized—and he could have kicked himself—that he still hadn't asked, straight out, what was in the closet. He didn't have much experience with people praying, but he could tell it was something that shouldn't be interrupted. He waited until, at last, Alex made the sign of the cross and stood up.

"Come on, Ewan," he said. "Let's go and meet my cousin. If anything worries you, just say the Lord's Prayer. There are old fears and hates hanging around here, but don't worry. They can't win."

At the top of the stairs, Alex made the sign of the cross again. Then, gently and calmly, as if he didn't want to frighten anyone, he opened the door.

"Elspeth?" he said softly. Ewan thought he had never heard such compassion and gentleness in any voice he had ever heard in his life. "Elspeth, dear, it's Alex. I'm here to help you."

He stepped into the room. Ewan followed him.

"She's normally at the window," he said.

"So she is," said Alex softly, "so she is. Little Elspeth."

Ewan saw her. She stood with her back to the window, the light behind her, eyes enormous in her pale face. Her gaze was fixed on Alex, yearning and terrified at the same time. She began to shiver. The room flashed into the 1930s, then back again.

"Are *you* a peterman?" she whispered. *"You?"*

"Yes, Elspeth."

"But I hate you!" she protested, but it seemed to Ewan that she didn't mean it. She might have hated her young cousin, but she didn't hate her peterman.

"You don't hate me, Elspeth," said Alex. "You hate what I told you, years ago. I am so, so sorry. I never meant to hurt you. Can you forgive me? It's time we cleared all that up, and you can be free. Will you let me put right the harm I did?"

He drew up a chair and sat down by the window. Ewan sat on the floor, and so—slowly, warily, with her eyes still on Alex's face—did Elspeth.

"Imagine this," he said. "A twelve-year-old boy going off to boarding school for the first time. Blazer, knee-length trousers, prickly collar. I didn't want to go. This was my home, and I felt I was being pushed out of it. I liked my own room, with plenty of space to have my things where I wanted them, especially my painting things. It was my space, and I had it just the way I liked it. The mess was my mess, the bed was my bed, and my paintings were my treasure. More than that—they were my heart and soul."

He took Elspeth's hand. Ewan wasn't sure how he did it, but he did.

"All of me was in my paintings," he said. "They seemed more real to me than the world around me. In a way, they were, because in my painting I was searching for something that was truer and stronger than the world I could see, something that couldn't be touched or seen or heard. Only felt."

Ewan thought of the way he felt when he stood at the top of the hill and looked over the loch. He thought of his father's lion.

"Those pictures were too precious to show people. I showed them my neat little landscapes and sketches, but not my special work. I would draw the same picture, over and over, but I could never get it quite as I wanted it."

"What did you draw?" asked Elspeth.

"A lion," he said. "My lion. I called him after the house. He became clearer and brighter every time I drew him, and his coat was like flame. Ninian, the Fire Lion."

The surprise made Elspeth's pale face glow as if she were alive. "That was my friend!" she said.

"Dad's lion!" said Ewan.

"Who thought of him first?" asked Elspeth. "You or me?"

"Maybe neither of us. Maybe somebody before us," said Alex, and smiled.

"But he wasn't real!" said Ewan, who felt he was losing the plot.

"That depends on what you mean by 'real,'" Elspeth said. "What we felt about him was real. So did you hide your paintings in the closet, Alex?"

"I had a wooden box that my grandfather had made for me to keep my treasures in. I put them in there and shut them in the closet so nobody could see them without my permission, but I felt uneasy about going away for a whole term and leaving them."

"I wish you'd told me," said Elspeth. "I would have kept them safe for you."

"Of course you would have," he said, pressing the hand that wasn't really there. "But I was twelve, pigheaded and scared. I came in here and saw my little cousin looking in the wardrobe. You did such a good job of staying out of everyone's way, Elspeth, I never really got to know you, and in those days, twelve-year-old boys without sisters didn't have a clue about girls. We weren't quite sure what they were, and we certainly didn't trust them. And the prospect of boarding school made a complete self-centered misery of me, I suppose. So when I found you looking in the wardrobe, you scared the daylights out of me! I was sure you'd be hunting about in the closet next. So, being a horrid young hooligan, I told you that story about an evil creature trapped in the closet. Believe me, Elspeth, I am so sorry. I never, ever meant to cause you such distress. If I had known, if I had known how long you've had to wait . . ."

"It's not your fault I caught diphtheria," she said. "And it's not your fault I got stuck in a time change."

"It's not just the time change, though, is it?" he said.

Elspeth looked at the floor for a long time. Ewan took the chance to get in the question he had wanted to ask.

"I don't understand," he said. "That closet's either locked or jammed solid. It won't open. She couldn't have touched your paintings. Or has it just become jammed since then?"

"It never locked, or jammed, and it still isn't locked," said Alex gently. He seemed to be speaking to Elspeth, not Ewan. "It isn't jammed. It never was, was it, Elspeth?"

She shook her head, and would not look at him.

"Why won't the closet open, Elspeth? You know, don't you? You've pretended not to know until you've convinced yourself. But, in your heart, you do know. What keeps the door locked?"

Ewan waited for the room to flicker back and forward in time, as it did whenever Elspeth was agitated. But it stayed perfectly still, though Elspeth's face was paler than ever and her eyes were huge. Tense and still, she met Alex's gaze. She did not flinch. When she spoke, it was a whisper, and each word was separate, like beads spread in a row, as if each one cost her a great effort.

"I'm so feart. I'm so scared of that closet."

"Well said, Elspeth." Alex still looked gravely into the wide gray-blue eyes. "So, tell me, in one word, *what keeps it shut.*"

There was a silence as if they were waiting for thunder. When it came, it was not thunder at all. It was a whisper.

"Fear," said Elspeth. Alex gave a quiet sigh of relief.

"Yes," he said. "It's fear. Perfect love is stronger than fear, Elspeth. And what else keeps the closet shut? What about the way you felt about me all those years?"

"You?" She looked steadily into his face. "I hated you."

"Can you forgive me?"

Elspeth said nothing. She only smiled as she had never smiled before.

Ewan looked from the pale face to the living one. Was this all that would happen? Would they sit here and smile peacefully at each other until Elspeth vanished into her singing, and Alex dashed off to America, and he would be left alone with the menacing closet? Whatever Alex had just said, the menace was real.

"Excuse me," he said urgently, "but you're saying Elspeth has imagined all this about the closet. There's really something there. Bruce was scared of it. *I* can feel it. And whenever I've tried to help Elspeth, even today, something's happened to get in the way."

"Tell him, Elspeth," said Alex.

"It's what I said before," said Elspeth. She turned to Ewan with concern in her face, as if she had hurt him and was sorry. "I didn't mean to do it. It's fear and hate. They got out of control. I didn't realize it myself until now. It's my own fear and hate that have trapped me and scared you. Nothing else. I'm sorry. I didn't realize they could be so strong."

"Not as strong as perfect love and forgiveness," said Alex.

Ewan shut his eyes. Something was about to happen. The whole room buzzed, hummed, and sang with it.

Alex crossed the floor and stood at the door of the closet. "Shall we let little Elspeth go, Ewan?"

Ewan understood. He pushed up the window, then crossed the room to the closet, to the door, which seemed larger and more solid than ever. If he thought about the thing he had to do, it would be too terrifying, so, knowing that Alex Sutherland was beside him, he just did it. The door flew open in his hand.

Too late to shut it again, too late, now he heard the rising, thundering roar and caught the flash of red eyes as something launched toward him. Then there was a little gasp or a cry from Elspeth, but it was a cry of delight as she saw what Ewan saw, though it was only for seconds. Golden as sunlight, joyous as victory, the fiery shape of a lion sprang from the closet—and was it a lion, or a ray of golden light that flashed past him and out through the open window? He shut his eyes against the brightness and heard singing, or flowing water, or both, and music so lovely it was unbearable, and a child laughing and laughing.

When he opened his eyes, the bedroom was just a bedroom. Any old bedroom, with the window and a closet door open.

Suddenly he felt empty and unhappy. It was as if he had been deprived of a treasure. Everything had become flat. Alex put a hand on the shoulder that didn't hurt.

"We never said good-bye properly," said Ewan. "There were still things I wanted to say to her."

"She's free," said Alex. "That's what really matters."

Ewan leaned out the window, as if he could wave to her, though he knew it was impossible. He drew his head back, pulled down the window, and noticed something at his feet.

Alex had seen it, too. Ewan picked it up.

"What beautiful lichen!" said Alex. "Wasn't Elspeth . . . ?"

"Yes," said Ewan. "I gave it to her. Now she's left it for me." And now he felt that she really had said good-bye, and was free.

- 12 -

Ewan sat on his bed, rubbing his sore shoulder with one hand and holding the lichen twig with the other.

"You may as well see," said Alex, who was still at the closet. With the door open, it looked like a gaping, toothless mouth. When Ewan peered in, it smelled of cobwebs, spiders, and mustiness. There was a wide, shallow box in there, a wooden one.

"Be my guest," said Alex. He drew it out and put it on the floor.

Ewan thought the clasps would be too rusty to open, but they were hardly even shut. He lifted back the lid and took out the yellowing, curling pictures inside.

"It's him!" Asonished again, he raised his eyes to Alex's face. "The lion. He really was in here!"

Alex lifted out the pictures one by one, smiling at them with affection. There was the lion in full flight, as Ewan had just seen him. Another one showed him rearing up to paw the air, and in the next his head was thrown back, as if he was roaring.

"If I'd done these pictures, I'd have come back for them," said Ewan. "Why did you just leave them there?"

"By the time I came home from school, I had more ideas about drawing," said Alex. "New styles and subjects to try. When I first did these, they were very precious to me, but I moved on. Pity, though. I *should* have come back for them. Perhaps I was a bit afraid of the closet, too."

Ewan began to say something, and stopped.

"Did you want to ask something else?" suggested Alex.

He did, but he wasn't sure how to. "You know," he said, "the lion . . ."

"The one that jumped out of the closet?" said Alex casually, as if lions flew out of closets all the time. "Of course, he wasn't really a lion. That was, in a way, a picture of something good—something in Elspeth, in you, in me—that's been trapped by fear and resentment all this time. A picture of something invisible. Poor Elspeth was scared of her own shadow. Oh, Ewan, the treasures we keep locked away!"

"But why a lion? You and Elspeth imagined a lion here. So did my dad."

"Somebody must have imagined him first. And this place has always been good at showing secrets that any sensible house would keep hidden. The lion just appeared, the way scenes from the past appear. Perhaps the man downstairs thought of him before anybody else did."

The only man downstairs was Ewan's dad, who, by the

sounds coming from the kitchen, had just gotten home, but Ewan knew that wasn't who Alex meant. "Which man downstairs?" he asked.

"Haven't you seen him?" It was the first time Alex had found anything surprising. "Oh, you will. I'm sure you will. I *hope* you will." He straightened up. "If you'll excuse me, I'll go and say blessings on the house, just to tidy it up. Those old Scots warriors gathering in the hall always look a bit scrappy, don't they?"

Ewan shut the closet door and, just to check that it still worked, opened and shut it a few times more. He was already wondering why he had ever been afraid of it. Then he gathered up the sheaf of old pictures, holding them with great care, and carried them downstairs.

"Where did you find those, Ewan?" asked his father. He rubbed his hands on his shirt and looked over Ewan's shoulder at the pictures.

"Alex did them when he was twelve. He left them in a closet in my bedroom. The one that was jammed, except it isn't. Alex opened it."

"He must be some kind of peterman!" said his mother, and laughed. She stopped laughing when she saw Ewan's face. "Is everything all right?"

Ewan nodded, and forgot how old he was, and leaned against her. "It's all empty now," he said. "The closet, I mean."

Ewan's mother gave him an odd look, but he didn't explain further.

It was a relief to know he could get changed in his own bedroom now that Elspeth wasn't there. But he missed her already. He'd become used to her.

"There, that's better!" Alex strode briskly into the kitchen. "Simon, it's awfully cheeky to ask, I know, but is there any chance at all that I could see the studio, or workshop, or hole in the ground, or wherever it is that you work?"

For Ewan's father, this day was getting better and better, and he swung open the door to the cellar. Ewan followed them down the stone steps and was halfway down when he and Alex saw the same thing. He stopped and caught his breath.

The lion was nearly completed. He was balanced on a stand to hold him in place, as his forepaws were lifted in a spring. His mane and coat were not, this time, made of flame but of dried leaves and grasses and bark. He looked wholly alive, and he was beautiful.

Alex looked back over his shoulder and grinned at Ewan.

"He gets everywhere, doesn't he?" he said.

Ewan sat on the steps while the two men toured the studio, Alex making admiring remarks and commenting on half-finished pieces. At some point they started to talk about galleries, but Ewan didn't take it in. He only gazed at the lion, and the more he gazed, the more it seeemed wonderful, the way each curling leaf and each crumble of lichen was part of the whole, leaping, glorious figure. It was like a feast to stay still and gaze at Ninian the Lion.

At last the two men came back up the steps, and he joined them. At the top, they all turned for a last look at Ninian.

Ninian was not to be seen. The sculptures, the tools, the rolls of wire mesh and boxes of clutter had vanished. All that was left was the bare room, warm with the dim light of a burning torch on the wall and the smoky glow of candles. A wooden cross stood on a stone altar, and on the ground before it, with his back to them, knelt a man in a gray tunic. His hair had been shaved at the crown, but hung long and straggling at the back. His strong, bony hands were clasped, his eyes were closed, and in a soft, measured voice he repeated words in Latin. The words, falling slowly and separately like drops of candle wax, carried such profound calm that Ewan ached to be near him, as if the monk radiated peace like warmth from a fire and exhaled it with his breath. And it seemed as if the monk praying underground in the ancient chapel and Elspeth laughing her way through the open window and the bright lion were all one, and welcomed him in.

The studio became the studio again, and Ewan yearned for the hermit's chapel. But he found, as he turned away, that it was still there inside him.

Steadily, day by day, Ewan found he could cope with missing Elspeth. Every week, then every day, winter came closer and was more of a threat. Sometimes the storms were so bad and the rains so torrential that even the journey to Mick's house was too dangerous to try. Ewan's headmaster questioned why Ewan couldn't get to school when Mick managed to, unaware that the long loch-side path became flooded between Ninian House and the rest of Loch Treen.

The news that Alex Sutherland had discovered an exciting new sculptor spread quickly around the art world. Galleries and collectors were in competition to buy the works of Simon Dart. *Ninian the Lion* was not for sale, though Simon did lend him to an exhibition. Lizzie worried that she had so much work she'd have to turn clients away. Ewan was glad, very glad, that Elspeth was free, but Ninian House was lonelier than ever without her.

Mick's family came to the rescue. "We'll have Ewan over anytime," they said, and he was glad of it. He'd always liked Mick's family, and Mick was the kind of friend who accepted you just the way you are. Just as important, he was a friend who could be seen and who wasn't about to disappear out of a window into the air. But Ewan kept the lichen branch. He'd always keep that.

On a rainy evening when the dining room fire had been lit, Ewan told his parents about Elspeth. He felt he needed to. She was such a big part of his life, even now that she'd gone. When he'd finished, his mother put her arm around him and asked why he hadn't told them before, but Ewan couldn't answer that. He didn't exactly understand it himself.

• • •

He knew his parents were working up to something one Saturday evening. They had all sat down to an extremely nice meal of lasagna with lots of cheese, followed by fudge ice cream, and they seemed to want to linger at the table. There just happened to be three mini chocolate bars in the refrigerator, so they ate those with their coffee.

"You like it here, don't you, Ewan?" said his mother.

Ewan wondered what they wanted him to say. It sounded like a first step toward moving house.

"I love it," he said. "I wouldn't want to live anywhere else. I like the house and the way it carries the past around with it, and I love the loch and the hill. It'll be cold in winter, and I'm not looking forward to that, and it's a pity it's so far from anywhere. It's too far to have friends calling round, and I really miss that. But I don't want to leave."

His parents exchanged glances across the table.

"I don't think we've been fair to you," said his mother. "Dragging you off to the back of beyond like this. It's solitary confinement."

"It's Ninian House," he said, and he found he was ready to fight for it. "Yes, it's lonely, and that isn't easy, but it's where we belong."

"Tell you what we've been thinking." Mum put down her coffee cup and rested her elbows on the table. "Summers here aren't bad, I know, but the winters will be far worse than we realized."

No, thought Ewan, but she went on.

"Your father and I are both doing so well all of a sudden, we've got real money coming in. Plenty of it. We don't have to shiver in a drafty barn all winter."

No, no, no.

"What we could do with," she said, "is somewhere small that we can rent for the winter. We can afford that now. Somewhere nearer to the village so you won't have a long walk home from the bus when it's snowing, and in the meantime . . ."

"NO!" The fight burst out from Ewan. "We live here, and I love it, and it's where we have to be! I want to have Christmas here! This is where we belong!"

His mother looked at him in astonishment. "Who said any different?" she said. "Of course we'd still live here. But if we rented something as well, we'd have a halfway house for when the weather's really bad. I've been looking forward to Christmas in Ninian House, too."

Suddenly it seemed too good to be true. Ewan knew that adults have a way of squashing a perfect idea, but he said what was in his mind.

"Mick's mum hasn't got a winter tenant for the cottage." He thought of winter evenings with Mick and Bruce. Remote-controlled cars. Videos. Granny Carmichael. Being part of a big, muddly family. No more trudging all the way home in hailstorms. "She wants a long winter tenant. You should ask her."

"I already did," said Mum, and smiled smugly into her coffee.

"We haven't booked it yet," said his father. "We told her we would if you liked the idea. What do you think?"

Dazed with happiness as he gave his answer, Ewan wondered why it was that things were suddenly turning out so well, as if all the right doors were opening. Was it because of Elspeth, or Alex the peterman? Or Ninian the Lion, or the monk in the chapel, or even himself? Whoever and whatever it was, he was glad to bursting.

"Where are you off to?" called his mother as he ran to the door.

"I'm going to tell Mick!" he yelled back. And as he ran full pelt along the loch side, he felt as if he were Ninian the Lion, carried by fire and laughter, leaping into the sky.